Scars

Matthew Storm

ACKNOWLEDGMENTS

Many thanks to Michele, for reading yet another of my painfully bad drafts.

Also thanks to Banks, MS MR, S.J. Tucker, Lindsey Stirling, M83, and Kosheen, for the soundtrack.

Chapter 1

I'd been thinking about killing myself for half an hour when my cell phone rang and Sarah Winters asked if I'd come out and look at a crime scene. "It might be *him*," she said. I figured I might as well. I could always kill myself later if I couldn't come up with anything better to do.

The body was in Hillcrest, a small neighborhood just north of downtown known for its restaurants and nightlife. I parked next to an ambulance and got out of my Mustang, putting a hand inside my black leather jacket to check that my Glock was still there as I stood up. I'd known it was there, of course, tucked away in its shoulder holster. It was *always* there. That knowledge never stopped me from making sure of it, though. I'd gotten obsessive over it recently. Not that anyone in their right mind could blame me.

The moon was high and clouds were rolling in from the sea as I locked the Mustang's door behind me. The wind felt cool and moist, as if it might rain, but it probably wouldn't. San Diego was a tease that way. I loved the city, but the weather was as predictable as a Swiss watch. There were times I would have killed someone if it meant we could get a good storm for a change. Well, maybe not *killed*. Slapped around a little, maybe. That didn't seem too unreasonable.

I looked around for a moment before heading for the line of yellow tape that had been set up to cordon off the alley. A small crowd had gathered nearby and a white television news van with an array of electronics on its roof had parked just behind them. A camera crew was already setting up lights and a reporter would be on camera soon. They couldn't have much yet, unless they'd been tipped off to the fact that this might not be just any other murder. If they hadn't been, *my* presence here was going to be a big clue as to what was going on. It was still early enough that they might get their report onto tonight's ten o'clock news. Then again, if this turned out to be what the media no doubt wanted it to be, they might be willing to break into *America's Super Teenage Singing Extravaganza*, or whatever it was that people were watching these days. A serial killer who had gone silent, only to resurface some three and a half years later, might even get national coverage.

The SDPD uniforms guarding the alley didn't bother asking for my ID. I wasn't a cop anymore, but there was little doubt every cop in the city would recognize me. Fame is a funny thing. Cops tended to act like I was some kind of mythological figure; something people talked about but never expected to actually see. That could either work for or against me, of course. Plenty of people were probably happy when Perseus chopped the Medusa's head off. But others probably thought Perseus might be a bit of a loose cannon, and wondered when he was going to flip out and kill *them*.

"Detective," one of the uniforms nodded at me, holding

2

the yellow tape up for me to pass under. I didn't bother to correct him. Dan Evans, my old boss, had told me once a cop, always a cop. I nodded back at the uniform and started down the alley.

The body was under a white sheet next to an overfilled dumpster. The CSI guys had finished up, then, and they were just waiting for somebody to come and cart the body off. But then I noticed two of the medical examiner's guys waiting a few yards away next to a stretcher. One of them was smoking a cigarette. I hadn't realized anyone in California still smoked. But that meant Sarah had made them wait for me. That had been sweet of her. Probably unnecessary, but still sweet.

Sarah was easy to spot in these surroundings, there being a distinct lack of pretty blonde women standing around the body. She wore a dark belted coat with boots of some stylish design I'd never have been able to name. Everything I knew about style could be written on the back of a postcard and then set on fire for all I cared about it. She was speaking to a man I didn't know but left him when she saw me coming. "Nevada," she said. "It's good to see you."

"Hey, Sarah," I nodded. Sarah Winters had been new to the Homicide Division back when I'd been on the Laughing Man case. She'd been around to see my implosion and the end of my career. Sometimes I didn't know why she still talked to me, but then again, I didn't really understand why *anyone* still talked to me. Nobody outside of Oscar the Grouch would have called me a ray of sunshine. I was more the type people crossed the street to avoid.

"Thanks for coming," she said. "I wasn't sure if…" she hesitated and looked at me as if I was a puzzle she was trying to solve. "I mean, I thought maybe you'd be busy, or…"

I didn't need to be Sherlock Holmes to know the question she really wanted answered. It would probably be easier to show her rather than tell her. I dug into the front pocket of my dirty jeans, pulled out a small plastic medallion, and handed it to her. Her eyes widened just a bit as she read the text printed there, and I allowed myself one brief instant of pride. Just one, though. I managed to catch the smile that was trying to reach my mouth and pound it back into submission before she noticed.

"Three months?" Sarah asked. "You've got three months?"

"And a few days more, now. One day at a time, as they say." I hated A.A. clichés. I hated them even more when they happened to be true.

I waited for her to hand the medallion back, but her lip trembled and then she stepped forward and threw her arms around me, nearly making me lose my balance. "Okay, I guess we're doing this," I said. Sarah was a hugger. I wasn't. I patted her once on the back, thinking that this might be the signal that we were done hugging now. It wasn't. She held on for a good ten seconds before letting me go.

"I'm so proud of you," she said, wiping a tear away from one eye.

"Yeah, well…thanks," I said as she handed the medallion back. "It's really not a big deal."

"It's a *very* big deal," she said. "I really thought we were going to lose you."

"Still might," I shrugged. "The night is young."

The man Sarah had been speaking with earlier had been loitering a few feet away. Now he stepped forward. "You must be Nevada James," he said. "The prodigal daughter returns." He held out a hand to shake.

"Do you know what *prodigal* means?" I asked.

His hand stayed suspended in the air like it was attached to a helium balloon. "Um…it means the one who left."

"No," I said. "It means wasteful, or extravagant. It could also mean overly abundant. It's got nothing to do with me, though."

"Oh," he said. He put his hand down.

Sarah cleared her throat. "Nevada, this is my partner. Brad Ellis. Brad, meet Nevada."

Ellis was about six feet tall and looked like a dumbass Ken doll. Or maybe I was just annoyed with him. It was definitely one or the other. He had close-cropped blond hair and I knew he hadn't bought his sport coat at the Men's Wearhouse. It looked like it had been sewn around his body while he stood there and preened in the mirror. I tried to think of something clever to say, but I'd worn myself out defining the word *prodigal* for him. "Nice to meet you," I said.

"Yeah," he nodded. "It's going really well so far."

I looked back at Sarah. "So what have you got?"

"Male vic, Caucasian, early thirties…" Ellis started.

"Sarah?" I asked, ignoring him.

Sarah shot Ellis a look that said *you should probably shut up now* in no uncertain terms. "Male victim, Caucasian, early thirties. Single stab wound in the back of the neck as the cause of death. Looks like it was a small blade, maybe four inches, but we'll know more later. It's consistent with a Laughing Man kill." She nodded at the covered body. "Lips and surrounding skin removed postmortem to make the smile."

That last part was the Laughing Man's signature mutilation. He'd done it to all his victims, the last one as I'd watched. I'd seen it more times than I cared to count.

I nodded. "I'm going to take a look."

One of the medical examiner's guys pulled back the sheet when he saw me coming. He didn't need to ask who I was, either. A while back he'd wheeled a body out of my house; there had been a hit out on me and the guy who had come to snuff me wound up with a broken trachea. I hadn't meant to kill him. Sometimes shit just happened.

The man on the ground probably was in his early thirties, but I wasn't great at guessing ages. I'd take Sarah's word for it. He was lying face-up now so I couldn't see the neck wound, but that wasn't what I was here for, anyway. I knelt down to take a close look at his face. The medical examiner looked away while I turned the victim's head so I could see both sides clearly. I'd have had to admit it was fairly gruesome, but this wasn't new to me. The man's lips had been cut off and a triangle of skin leading back to where his jaw hinged trimmed away on each side. The exposed teeth gave him the semblance of a wide grin, although a grotesque one.

I'd seen all of this I needed to see. I stood back up and nodded at the medical examiner, who draped his sheet over the body again and stepped away. I took a look up and down the alley. There wasn't a great deal to see, other than the dumpster and the normal trash scattered around that you'd expect. A pile of flattened cardboard boxes lay not far away next to a shopping cart full of plastic bags stuffed with God knew what.

I heard a step behind me. Sarah stood there, with Ellis just behind her. Ellis didn't look all that pleased with me. He'd probably assumed meeting me would be a different kind of experience. In all fairness I'd probably been too hard on him, but I hadn't cared much for his tone. Prodigal daughter, my ass.

"What do you think?" Sarah asked.

I looked back at the covered body and shrugged. "What do *you* think, Sarah?"

She looked at the covered body for a moment, hesitating, as if she could see it through the sheet and find the clue she needed to answer me before she spoke. Then she met my eyes again. "It's a copycat."

"It's a copycat," I nodded. "How do you know?"

Sarah bit her bottom lip. "The marks on the face aren't clean enough," she said. "Not precise enough, I mean. When we get the report, I'm betting it says the cuts were made with a knife. Not a straight razor like *he* uses."

"Good," I said. "What else?"

"What else?" Ellis asked. "Fair enough, the cuts weren't done right, but what else are you looking for here?"

"Art," I said. "The Laughing Man is an artist. It's important to him."

"It's not really what I'd call art," Sarah said quietly.

"I didn't say I wanted to see it in the fucking *Louvre*," I said, "but it's still art. This body isn't posed. There's no *scene* here. There's no story. When the Laughing Man kills someone, that's just the medium he works in. You see this?" I nodded at the body. "This is just some trash in an alley."

"Jesus *fucking* Christ," Ellis said.

That hadn't come out exactly right. "I mean, it's terrible that a guy died, of course." I was perfectly aware of how sincere I didn't sound, but there wasn't much to be done about it. "But whoever did this is just a garden-variety murderer with delusions of grandeur. He's just a fan who wants to be the real thing. It's not the Laughing Man."

"Thanks, Nevada," Sarah said. "I'm sorry we dragged you all the way out here."

"No, don't be. It was the right call. I'd have been pissed if you found this and *didn't* call me. One of these days he's going to start the game again. It's just not today."

That was what the Laughing Man had told me when he reappeared in my life three months ago. He'd missed the game. He wanted a rematch. And I was the only person he wanted to play with.

Sometimes I wondered what the hell he was waiting for.

"I'm surprised Dan's not here," I said. Dan was the captain of the SDPD's homicide division, my old boss and probably my best friend. Not that there was a lot of competition in that department. He took anything potentially involving the Laughing Man very seriously.

"He's visiting his mother in Santa Fe," Sarah said. "I didn't think I should call him until we knew what we were looking at."

"Probably for the best," I said. "If he thought the Laughing Man was active again he'd have run all the way here. Anyway, check with the homeless guy who lives over there." I pointed at the shopping cart and flattened boxes. "He'll come back eventually. I doubt he saw anything, but you never know."

"We did notice the shopping cart," Ellis said.

"Just remember he's not the *prodigal* homeless guy," I said. Ellis scowled at me. "Oh, come on," I protested. "That was funny!"

Ellis turned and walked away. "Sorry," I said to Sarah.

"Forget it," she said. "He's a decent guy, really. He thinks he's hot shit, though."

I made an expression of mock horror. "Sarah! Did you just say *shit*?"

She smirked. "I did."

"I don't think I've ever heard you swear before."

"It's not a habit of mine. I do know the words, though."

I looked back at the body on the ground. They were getting ready to hoist the victim onto a stretcher and take him away. "I do appreciate the call. When you see Dan, tell him I haven't forgotten about him sending over my case files."

"I thought he sent them already?"

"He left a few out," I said. "The ones he doesn't want me looking at because he thinks I'll start having flashbacks and flip out. He'll know which ones they are."

She nodded. "Your last case. I know that one, too." She squinted at me. "You wouldn't start flipping out, would you?"

"Would anyone know the difference if I did?"

She didn't answer that question, looking back at Ellis, instead. He was talking with the two uniforms at the end of the alley. Maybe he was giving them a vocabulary lesson. "So how would you tackle this?" she asked.

I shrugged. "I wouldn't bother."

"Nevada!" She looked like I'd just slapped her face.

"Oh," I said, "I don't mean just let the guy go. But you're not going to catch him before the Laughing Man does."

Sarah gave me a look as if I'd told her to start her investigation by building a rocket ship and flying to the moon to look for clues there. "What are you talking about?"

"Didn't I already explain this?" I asked. The look she gave me suggested I hadn't. "The Laughing Man is an artist."

"And?"

"And he takes his work seriously. Very seriously." I frowned. "I'm not sure it's something I can explain very well. It would be like if you were Michelangelo and you caught some guy doing crayon drawings on the wall of the Sistine Chapel and signing your name to them."

She nodded. "That's a terrible analogy. I get what you mean, though."

"Okay," I said, "so as soon as this hits the television news, which will probably be about…" I looked toward the end of the alley where I could see a cameraman trying to get a shot, "five minutes from now, he's going to start looking for whoever did this. It won't be a job for him like it is for the police. It'll be an obsession. And in the end, whoever did this is going to wind up in one of his still lifes." I thought it over. "It'll probably be something that suggests the copycat was stupid, or childish. You might find the body in a school. Art class, maybe. I don't know."

Sarah stared at me. "If I didn't know better, I might think *you* were the Laughing Man."

"Good thing you do know better, then." I shrugged. "I don't have a lot to do until he starts the game again. I think about him pretty much…yeah, all the time."

"You need to get out more," Sarah said. "Come have a drink with me sometime…" she caught herself almost immediately and I could see her face flush. "God, I'm sorry, I don't mean have a *drink*."

"Damn it, Sarah, do you want me to relapse?"

"I'm so sorry, Nevada, I…"

I held up a hand. "I was kidding. Forget it."

She sighed. "I just meant it's not good for you to be sitting around obsessing over him all the time."

"Could be worse," I said. "I could be obsessing over him and drinking."

Chapter 2

Two of the SDPD uniforms kept the media off of me as I walked back to my Mustang. The reporters were swarming around like flies on shit now, shouting questions about the Laughing Man and asking if that was why I'd been called to the crime scene. I ignored them. I hadn't answered a reporter's questions since I'd been a cop, and even then I hadn't done it very well. I wasn't about to start again now. The police would make a statement of their own soon enough, and once they'd established that it wasn't the Laughing Man who had done the killing, nobody would want to ask me anything anymore. I preferred it that way.

I wondered how long it would be before the Laughing Man heard the news. I almost wished I could be there to see his reaction. He'd probably be apoplectic. It would give me something to chuckle about right before I put a bullet in his skull.

Three months ago I'd been a drunk living in a rented house in Ocean Beach, a quiet suburb in the southwest part of San

Diego. I'd have been content to live out the rest of my short life there, drinking myself to death as quickly as I could manage, but a local crime boss named Alan Davies had offered me a great deal of money to investigate the kidnapping of his wife and daughter. That had led to two people dying in my house in the span of a few days. The first had been the would-be assassin who had been sent to kill me. The second had been the man behind the abductions, a lawyer named Chandler Emerson. When I'd exposed him, he'd expressed his unhappiness by hitting me with a Taser and then duct-taping me to a chair. He would have tortured me to death but then, three years after our last meeting, the Laughing Man had returned. He'd been watching me the whole time, waiting to see what I'd do, but when he realized he was about to lose his playmate forever he'd struck, cutting Emerson's throat and then creating a still life right there in my dining room. He'd set places for us at my table and then posed us, me still taped to a chair, like a happy couple sitting down to eat dinner.

And then the Laughing Man had offered me a choice. I could either die right there, or he'd let me live and we'd play the game again. I'd spent the three years since our last meeting trying to kill myself with vodka, and I'd have been lying if I'd said dying right there hadn't sounded like a relief after all that time. But I'd have been damned if he was going to be the one to kill me. I'd chosen to play the game again, and I'd told him so. I still remembered how happy he'd sounded at the time, even with his voice distorted through the Greek theatre mask he always wore when he was working.

After that I hadn't much wanted to live in that house anymore. Given that I knew the elderly couple I'd been renting it from would never be able to sell it after the killings, I'd taken some of the money I'd been paid for working the Davies kidnapping and bought it from them. Then I'd had the whole place torn to the ground. A new house was under construction for me there, but its completion was still a few months away. I'd been living in a small motel in Mission Valley since then. It was nothing fancy, offering little more than a queen size bed, a television, and a kitchenette, but it was all I needed, and the price was right. I'd been paid enough for that last job that I wasn't going to need money anytime soon. And now that I wasn't spending every dime that came my way on alcohol, I didn't have a lot in the way of expenses.

I drove one long loop around the motel before parking in the lot out front. I'd made it a point to check regularly for anything that looked out of place since the Laughing Man had come into my house. In the three years I'd been a drunk he'd checked in every now and then, sending greeting cards on my birthdays and holidays, and even had flowers delivered on rare occasions. Up until he'd cut Chandler Emerson's throat in my dining room, though, I'd never realized the extent of his attentions. He'd been watching me up close and personal. There was little doubt he knew where I was staying now, and little doubt I'd seen him at least once in his civilian guise since then. I had no idea what he looked like under his mask, though. But if I saw the same guy loitering in a parked car more than once, I'd be stopping him to ask some questions.

Once inside my room I turned on the television to a local news station and opened the dresser drawer where I had a bottle of vodka stashed. I poured half an inch into one of the cheap plastic cups the motel provided and sat down on the bed. The lead story on the news was the alley murder I'd just come back from. Sarah and Brad Ellis were wrapping up a press conference, stating flatly that this wasn't a Laughing Man murder. Someone had obviously tipped the press off to the signature slicing on the victim's face. The word *copycat* was being used. If the Laughing Man wasn't also watching this right now, he'd see it soon enough.

I raised the cup and sniffed the vodka as a wild-eyed reporter speculated on what all of this could *mean*, as if a dead man in an alley could carry subtext like something in one of Shakespeare's plays. The smell of the alcohol made my stomach turn and I had to suppress my gag reflex as my mouth started to water. The urge to drink was never far away from me. I wasn't sure why I tortured myself like this every night, except for that somehow *not* having the booze available would have been even worse. I hadn't taken a sip in over three months, but I still had to have a bottle nearby. It was a kind of security blanket, as crazy as that sounded.

I turned the television on to some mindless sitcom I didn't know the name of and eyed the stack of file boxes I'd lined up against the wall near the bathroom. They contained the Laughing Man case files I'd put together while I'd been a cop; the ones I'd insisted Dan send over for me to review. He'd left the last one out, the case where I'd been too late to save the Laughing Man's final victims, two little girls that he'd already killed and posed in a still life by the time I got to the scene. And then the Laughing Man had beaten me half to death, breaking my wrist and ribs with a crowbar before going to work on me with his hands. Dan probably hoped I'd forget about that case. I wouldn't. I'd never forget about it.

The smell of the vodka wafted up from the plastic cup as I swirled it around. I looked at it for another minute, then went to the sink and poured it down the drain. The bottle went back in the drawer. I'd do this ritual again tomorrow. I did it every night.

My cell phone buzzed. The number on my caller ID was one I knew pretty well. I could ignore it, but I knew he'd just call back until he got an answer, so I picked it up. "Hi, Paul."

"Hello, Nevada," he said. Paul had been Sarah's training officer back when she was a rookie. These days he was retired and ran an A.A. meeting for cops and ex-cops. He had a voice like some wise old grandfather figure. When I'd met him the first time I'd been half drunk and his kindly tone kind of made me want to punch him in the face. I'd gotten over that.

"I wonder why you're calling," I said. "It's almost as if you're checking up on me, but I don't know how *that* could be the case..."

"I saw you on the news," he said.

I'd assumed he'd just seen the news, but I didn't know I'd been on it. "They ran a shot of me?"

"They had a loop of you getting into your car. They only repeated it thirty or forty times."

"Must be a slow news night," I said.

"Well, not really. I expected you to call. Are you all right?"

"I'm fine."

"Somehow I doubt that, Nevada."

"I'm not drinking, if that's what you're worried about."

"That's part of it," Paul said, "but the bigger issue is whether you're okay."

I considered brushing him off, but experience had taught me that wasn't going to get me very far with him. He'd just call back again and again until I'd told him something he felt was *real.* "It wasn't the Laughing Man," I said. "It's just some asshole with a knife and delusions of grandeur. But yes, I'm okay. I'd be okay if it was the Laughing Man, too. I'd just be hunting tonight instead of standing on the sidelines watching..." I glanced at the television, "whatever the hell this is. Is there a sitcom about two guys who run an airline?"

"I don't know. Am I going to see you in group tomorrow?"

"Probably not."

"I think you should come in."

"Let me check my calendar," I said. I paused for a moment. "Nope, I've got some important staring at the ceiling to do. Can't make it."

I could hear him restrain a chuckle before it made its way out of his mouth. "Don't you think it would be good for you to talk, Nevada?"

"Not really."

"Then don't you think it would be good for you to listen?"

I sighed. This was going nowhere. "Look, Paul, I appreciate the group. I really do. But I'm a big girl. I'm not going to run out and down a bottle every time I think about the Laughing Man. Because that would be *every day.* Tonight's not different than any other night, except for the fact I had to get out of my room for an hour and go look at a dead guy. It was nice to break my routine up, really."

Paul was silent for a moment. "Well, you're going to do whatever you're going to do, Nevada. I do hope you'll come to a group soon, though. If you can't do it for yourself, then do it for the others."

"Oh, god, not this again. Please don't start telling me how I help other people with their struggles, Paul. I can't handle it."

"I'll let it go for tonight," he said, "but that doesn't mean I'm wrong. Your being at group isn't just about you, Nevada."

"So you've said before," I told him. "I'm going to hang up on you now."

"You have my number. I want you to call me before you do anything you're going to regret, though. Do you respect me enough that you can tell me you will?"

I rolled my eyes, but then remembered he couldn't actually see me. "You are the master of the guilt trip," I said. "Lucky for me I'm immune to it." He waited. "I'm not making any promises, Paul. I have your number, though."

"I'll take that. Good night, Nevada."

"Good night." I clicked the phone off.

I thought about what Paul had said for a few minutes. I went to group once a week, most weeks, but I'd never felt like I was a part of it. Maybe I had a bit of the old unwillingness to join any group that would have me as a member. That had been Groucho Marx's excuse. I'd gone in to get my three-month medallion, though, so it had to have meant something to me.

And it wasn't really like I had a lot else to do. Maybe I'd just show up because nobody expected me to. That would teach them a lesson. Or something.

I took my gun out of its shoulder holster and held it in my hands for a minute. The urge I'd felt earlier, the one that told me to put the barrel in my mouth and pull the trigger, had faded. I sighed. It would come back. I probably wouldn't do it

18

the next time, either. I didn't exactly have a lot to live for, but I really did want to put a bullet in the Laughing Man before I died myself.

My phone buzzed again, a text message this time. It was Sarah. She'd typed *ARE YOU OKAY???* in all caps and using three question marks so I'd know it was important, apparently. *I'm fine*, I sent back. I was beginning to think I'd need to shut my phone off if I was going to get any sleep tonight, but enough people knew where I was staying that I might risk being woken up by a frantic knock at the door if I stopped responding to messages. Having people care about you could be a real pain in the ass at times.

I put my gun on the nightstand where it sat every night and watched part of another sitcom, and then the beginning of a late-night talk show. My heart wasn't in either of them, though. In a way, I was disappointed that tonight's murder hadn't been the work of the Laughing Man, because at least it would have given me something to do. I knew that was a sick way to think, given that it meant he'd have begun a new killing spree, but it would also mean the game had started and I'd have new clues to work with. I'd caught up with him once, just over three years ago, but I hadn't been ready for him then. I wouldn't have lost our fight if I had been, and I certainly wouldn't have had a breakdown and wound up in the psych ward. And maybe I wouldn't have spent three years drinking myself into oblivion every day. This time I'd find him, kill him, and then I'd go to the cemetery in the middle of the night and dance on his grave. But to do any of that, I needed the game to start, and he was the only one of us who could say *go*. I'd been fooling myself thinking I'd find a clue that would lead me to him in my old case files. The Laughing Man didn't like to repeat himself. When the game started, it would be with something new. He'd want to show me something I hadn't seen before.

The game *would* start, though. I was willing to bet it would start soon. And I'd be ready for it.

Chapter 3

The local news was running a story on the Laughing Man copycat when I turned on the television the next morning. This time I caught the clip of myself getting into my car. It only ran once, fortunately. Hopefully that meant the media had accepted the idea that this wasn't a real Laughing Man case, which should cause interest in me to drop like a stone. I watched the rest of the story and shut the television off. I'd need to make a note to do a better job brushing my hair the next time there was a chance I might wind up on television. I didn't look like the wreck I'd been back when I was drinking, but I didn't look especially *good*, either.

I'd slept through two text messages, both of them from Dan Evans asking whether I was all right. I dashed off a quick reply that everything was fine. Knowing Dan, he was going to want to check in with me when he got back from Santa Fe. I didn't mind. It would give me a chance to pester him about the case files he hadn't given me.

Being unemployed and having very few friends and nothing

to do gave my days a certain empty flexibility that was both good and bad. While I had no responsibilities and nowhere I needed to be, I also tended to get extremely bored. I had considered trying to get a job, but my name carried a certain notoriety that made that difficult. Ever wondered what happened to Nevada James, the famous detective who lost her mind after the Laughing Man beat her half to death? She works at Macy's now. Let's go stare at her. There was also the fact that I hadn't exactly quit my last job; the SDPD had fired me. Not that I'd given them much of a choice. I'd tried going back after I'd gotten out of the hospital three years ago, but the phrase *bull in a china shop* came to mind. If the bull was rabid, anyway.

I spent a few minutes looking through the motel window for anything suspicious, then drove to the Denny's down the street for eggs and hash browns. I had simple tastes. On a day I was feeling really wild I might add some pancakes to the mix, but that was about all I ever did for breakfast.

My phone buzzed again as I was heading back to the motel. It was Jason London, a cop from Narcotics I knew from A.A. Narcotics guys didn't always get out clean, and Jason had been one of the unlucky ones. Percocet and cheap whiskey had been his thing. *Busy?* the text read.

I pulled the Mustang over so I could type without crashing into the back of another car. *You all right?* I didn't particularly enjoy it, but swapping phone numbers was part of what the group did. If someone had to make a choice between using and calling someone else for help, calling was always better. Even if it meant calling me, which I doubted was anyone's idea of a good time.

Fine. Friend asked to meet with you.

I frowned. That wasn't normal, and the timing couldn't have been a coincidence. *Reporter?*

No. Old friend needs some help. Will you meet?

Why?

Favor.

Don't recall owing you favor.

Please?

I thought it over. I wasn't a social person, and the only helping people I'd done recently was slipping homeless people twenty-dollar bills when they weren't looking. Then again, all I had to look forward to today was going back to my room and watching daytime television. Getting out for a little while would probably be good for me. It wasn't like I'd be too polite to get up and walk away if I got bored with the conversation.

Fine, I sent back. *When?*

Lunch?

Where?

Contradino's. 1:00 okay?

Done.

I put my phone back in my jacket pocket. Maybe I needed to change my number. I'd done more talking and texting in the last few months than I had in the entire three years previously. Then again, for a lot of that three years I hadn't even known where my cell phone *was*, and I'd been too drunk to care. Living in the 21st century wasn't going to kill me.

Contradino's was an Italian place in Point Loma, a neighborhood in the southwest tip of the city. It wasn't far from the house I'd been renting in Ocean Beach, and it was easy enough to find. As usual, I checked the rearview mirror more often than I needed to as I was driving, looking for any cars that might be following me. If I'd been doing that a year ago I'd have thought I was being paranoid, but that was before the Laughing Man had walked into my house seconds before Chandler Emerson started torturing me to death. He was out there, somewhere, and even if he wasn't watching me every day, I was sure he was never very far. Maybe one of these days I'd be able to make him. If I saw the same man too many times in one day in a city of over a million people…well, that might be a very interesting day. It was why my Glock was never more than an arm's length away.

Jason London was sitting in a booth near the door when I walked inside the restaurant. He was in his mid-forties but looked older. Substance abuse had done a number on his skin. He looked better than he had been when he was using, but had developed salt-and-pepper hair since then that wasn't doing him any favors. Some people just couldn't win.

Next to him sat a woman I guessed was in her sixties in a dark, three-button pantsuit. She was overdressed for Contradino's, which was more of a plastic tablecloth kind of place. She'd have stood out in a crowd regardless, though. About a third of the left side of her face had been badly burned at some point, probably at least a decade ago. The scars had healed well, and it looked like she'd had a world of expensive plastic surgery done, but there was a point with burns where all the skin grafts in the world were never going to make you look normal again. Whatever had happened to her, she'd never had a chance.

They stood up as I neared their table. "Nevada," Jason said.

"Thank you for coming."

"I wasn't that busy," I said. I looked at the woman. "Nevada James."

She extended a hand and I shook it. "I'm Anita Collins. It's so nice to meet you." She had a warm, singsong-y voice that made her sound like someone's grandmother in a Disney movie.

"Collins..." I said. "Have we met before? Your name sounds familiar."

"You're probably thinking of the Collins Foundation," she smiled. "I'm the Collins." She had such a joyful lilt in her voice I nearly checked the window to see if any birds were going to come sing us a song while we ate. None had appeared so far. It was still early, though.

If I'd been in the habit of admitting things, I'd have had to admit I was surprised that this was who Jason had wanted me to meet. The Collins Foundation was the parent group of a dozen or more charities in San Diego County. They funded everything from women's shelters to hospital expenses for sick children. Their name was printed on the jerseys of a local high school soccer team, if I remembered correctly. They'd funded the program after budget cuts had nearly eliminated it. I'd never met Anita, but it was no surprise I recognized her name. Half the population of San Diego had probably heard it at one time or another.

"Why don't we sit down?" Jason asked. "I ordered you a Diet Coke."

I didn't bother looking at the menu; I wasn't all that hungry yet after my breakfast. The soda was more than I'd need. Anita sipped a glass of iced tea and regarded me for a moment. "You look healthier than I expected, dear."

I nodded. "You thought I'd look half dead? I used to. You should have seen me three months ago."

"She looked like she'd crawled out of a grave," Jason said to her.

"It would be closer to say I was crawling *into* a grave," I said. "It seemed like a good idea at the time."

Anita smiled at me. "I hope I didn't offend you, dear. I'm just so pleased that you're better."

That was the second time she'd called me *dear*. If she hadn't sounded like she was going to whip out a magic wand and start granting wishes I'd probably have thrown something at her. "You didn't offend me. I saw the papers after the Laughing Man came to my house. Nothing about how they described me wasn't true."

"The *Gazette* called you a degenerate alcoholic," Jason said.

"See?" I asked Anita. "Who says you can't believe everything you read."

She smiled just a bit. "You're very frank," she said.

"That's because I don't care. Life's too short to go around pretending I'm not a complete fuck up." Jason's eyes widened a bit. "Sorry," I said. "I mean, a complete *screw* up. I'm not really used to making polite conversation." I shrugged. "So why am I here?"

Anita glanced at Jason, who nodded. "You know who I am, obviously. You know who my husband was, then?"

The waiter came by to take our orders. Jason ordered pasta.

Anita ordered a side salad. I decided against eating. When the waiter was out of earshot I said, "Adam Collins, if I remember right?" She nodded. "Half your charities have his name in them, or..."

"Stephen Collins is the other name. My son."

I let my brain roll that over a few times. "This would probably ring more of a bell for me if I hadn't spent the last three years trying to kill my brain with booze. Remind me?"

"You would have been very young when they were murdered."

I paused with my glass of Diet Coke halfway to my mouth and then sat it back down. "I do remember this, I think. A car bomb? Early 90's. It was some Unabomber shit. Stuff, I mean. Stuff."

Anita nodded. "It wasn't the Unabomber, but you have the right idea. My husband was a researcher at SDSU. He was a pioneer in artificial intelligence. And then someone put a bomb underneath our car in 1993."

"I know I must have read about that," I said. "I don't really remember, though."

"It was in the news quite a bit at the time. It fit the *modus operandi* of the Unabomber, and there had even been a warning note, but the FBI ruled him out." She looked away for a moment. "My husband and son died in the explosion. I survived, but..." she motioned at the burned portion of her face. "I'm sure you were wondering how this happened."

"I wasn't going to ask."

"I don't mind, dear. Like you, I am also very frank."

An alarm bell went off in my head. Was she pointing that out to try to make me identify with her? Or was it just that I was a remarkably paranoid person? I certainly *was* that, but… My hands were folded on the table in front of me. Hers were, as well. I spread my hands and put the right one on my lap, shifting my weight back in my seat. Two seconds later she did the same with her right hand and moved slightly back in her chair. I wasn't paranoid. She was mimicking me. It was an old body-language technique to build rapport with someone. She was clever. Maybe she wasn't such a kindly old grandmother, after all.

I thought about the case. "It was never solved, was it?"

"It was not," Anita said. "Which is why I asked Jason to introduce us."

I smirked. "Why do I think you're about to ask me to go look for the bomber?"

She smiled back. "Because your intuition serves you well. That's precisely what I'm asking."

I looked from Anita to Jason. He looked slightly embarrassed with himself. "Okay," I said. "I give up. Why are you asking *me*?"

"Because I saw you on television last night," Anita said. "It reminded me that you are a person who does not give up on things easily. You did have a reputation for being a rather dogged investigator. And also, I have been told that sometimes you are willing to work for people…how shall I say this…in something of an *unofficial* capacity?"

There were only so many places Anita could have found out what I'd done for Alan Davies. I shot Jason a nasty look and he suddenly found the table's salt shaker worthy of his undivided attention. "Imagine that," I said. "It's almost like someone here doesn't know what we talk about in group is supposed to stay in group."

"Jason didn't tell me where you met, but one doesn't have to be a detective to work that out. I do have eyes."

"That's not really the point," I said. Jason now seemed to find the pepper shaker very interesting. "What I said there never should have been repeated outside that room."

"Sorry," Jason murmured.

"He was only trying to help me," Anita said soothingly. "Please don't be angry with him."

I sighed. "Look, this is a twenty-year-old cold case." I rapped my knuckles on the table until Jason finally looked up at me. "When was the last time anyone reviewed it?"

"It's been inactive since 1995," Jason said. "It probably gets looked at once a year or so."

I nodded. He was probably being generous if he thought someone was actually looking at a case that had been dead that long once a year. "I'm sorry, but there's virtually no chance it's going to be solved now. It's been too long. There's no crime scene to investigate. I'm not going to discover any new evidence somebody else missed. Unless somebody just comes out of the woodwork and confesses, I wouldn't even know where to start with it."

"I think you said something similar about working a kidnapping," Anita noted. "And yet you managed to work that out."

I glared at Jason, who looked away again. "I got lucky."

"Maybe you'll get lucky again," Anita said. "I'm a very rich woman, Detective. I can pay you a great deal for your time."

"I'm not a detective anymore," I said. "I'm just someone who used to be one. And I have my own money."

"Will you at least think about it, Nevada?" Jason asked. "It's not like you have anything else to do."

"What I have to do is kick your ass the next time we're not in a restaurant full of witnesses."

"Fair enough," he said.

"Look, Mrs. Collins…" I started.

"Please call me Anita. I hope you'll let me call you Nevada?"

She did know how to use her charm. "Fine. The thing is, I'm all wrong for this. You should hire a private investigator. I could probably recommend someone if I thought about it for a while."

"I have hired private investigators. Nothing has ever panned out. I'd like to try someone new."

"Then you should look somewhere else. Me, I'm not what you want."

Anita tilted her head to the side. "Maybe I can decide for myself what I want. But I can only ask you to consider it. Would you do that? Consider it for a day or two? Is that too much for an old woman to ask?"

She was very good. Even though I knew I was being manipulated, her affect was enough to make me want to help her. When grandma tells you her back hurts because she's been working over a hot stove all day, you wind up eating her cookies even if she switched the sugar for salt. "I'll consider it, but that's going to be my answer tomorrow."

"We'll see," she said. She dug into her purse and came out with a small leather case from which she removed a business card. "There's my personal number." She offered me the card.

Against my better judgment, I took it. "I'm only saying I'll consider it, you understand?"

"Of course." The waiter came by with Jason's pasta and her salad. "Are you sure you don't want something to eat, Nevada?"

I stood up. "No. I have to get going. You'll hear from me."

"I'm looking forward to it," she smiled.

That made one of us.

Chapter 4

I drove in a loop of the freeways around San Diego after lunch, not really sure what to do with myself next. I kind of wanted to head north on I-5 and not turn back. I could do with some time out of the city. It was times like this I wished I had more friends.

After half an hour on the road I stopped at a Carl's Jr. and picked up a hamburger, but then wound up tossing it in the trash. I still wasn't hungry. The meeting with Jason and Anita hadn't sat right with me. Jason didn't need to be talking out of school the way he obviously had been, and as for Anita...there was something strange about her. It was hard to put my finger on, but I didn't like it.

I thought about heading back to my motel and kicking back for a while, but I didn't really have anything to do other than watch television or try and get Netflix working on my laptop over the motel's crappy Wi-Fi connection. I could hit Molly Malone's dojo for a workout, but I didn't really feel like sweating, either. For a minute I thought about buying plane tickets to Hawaii. I could sit on the beach and watch sunsets for a few days. What was stopping me? For that matter, what was stopping me from leaving this place and never coming back? I could start a new life somewhere else. I had the money for it. I could probably get myself a new identity, if I wanted to. I had enough contacts in the underworld to make that happen.

Thoughts like that tended to lead to me sitting on my bed holding my gun, though. It wasn't anything I wanted to dwell on today. In the end I just drove to a 7-11 to pick up snacks and some more Diet Coke. When I got back to my motel I saw Brad Ellis leaning up against his car in the parking lot. He walked over to me as I parked.

"Detective James," he nodded as I got out of the car.

"I'm not a detective anymore," I said. "You can just call me Nevada. Or Ms. James, if you like it better. I don't really care." I squinted at him. "How did you know where to find me?"

"Every cop in San Diego knows where to find you," Ellis said. "The captain has someone out here eyeballing the parking lot more nights than not."

That shouldn't have come as a surprise, but I was a little taken aback. Dan was going too far with that. I'd have to talk to him about it. "Oh," I said. "How about that."

"I wanted to apologize about last night," Ellis said. "We really didn't get off on the right foot."

I looked around the parking lot. "And you drove all the way over here to tell me that?"

He shrugged. "This place is literally five minutes away from the station."

"Okay," I said. "Forget about it. I probably didn't have to act like such a smartass, but…no, actually I did. Being a smartass is kind of my whole thing. Sorry."

He smiled. "Forget it."

"Anyway, I bought some chips. I have to go inside and eat them before they go bad."

Ellis looked as if he couldn't tell whether I was making a joke or not. "Yeah, okay."

He stood there as I swiped my keycard in the motel door's lock. I wondered if he thought I was going to invite him in. I wasn't, but just turning my back on him seemed awkward. "Was there something else you needed?" I asked.

Ellis looked like he was trying to do complex math in his head and for a minute I was afraid he was trying to work up the courage to ask me out. That wasn't going to end well. But instead he said, "Do you really think he's upset?"

"Who?"

"The Laughing Man," Ellis said. "About the homage. You think he's not going to see it that way? I'm asking because you know him better than anyone."

I thought about that. "Even if it was an homage, he's still going to see it as a cheap copy of his work. It's not like a Grateful Dead tribute band. Or maybe it is. I don't know what the Grateful Dead think about tribute bands. I'd be more inclined to think it was someone who wants to put his skills to the test, though. Not so much to honor the Laughing Man, but to compete with him."

"That's an interesting theory," Ellis said.

"Yeah, and I could be wrong. Maybe it's someone trying to audition. Somebody who's looking for attention. I never heard of a serial killer taking an apprentice, but maybe that's what your copycat is looking for. He's saying, 'Hey, I'm like you. Teach me.' But whatever the intention, if some guy shows up on your doorstep and hands you a bag of trash, you probably aren't going to be really happy about it."

"Trash," Ellis said, frowning at me.

I sighed. "Yeah, I know. It's a dead man and I'm a callous bitch because I can't stop talking like that. I've seen more bodies than I care to remember, Detective. I've put six of them in the ground myself. One more body in an alley is just...I'm numb to it. I know it should bother me. I know I'm broken. There's just not much I can do about it."

"I don't know," Ellis said. "There's therapy."

"I had a therapist once. It didn't really work out."

"Oh. I'm sorry."

"Nah, we're still tight. She's just not my therapist anymore. Anyway, I'm going inside now. You've got a copycat to catch. Good luck."

"Thanks," he said. "We'll get the guy, I'm sure."

"I'm sure you will. Sarah's smart as hell, and you...well, I don't know the first thing about you, but you seem to know what you're doing."

He held out his hand and this time I shook it. He'd been nice enough. It wouldn't kill me to be nice back to someone for a change. It wasn't like everyone I met was just waiting for a chance to stab me in the back, even though that was how I approached almost every new person I met these days. Maybe

I'd even make a new friend if I tried hard enough. And maybe pigs would fly out of my ass. That seemed a lot more likely.

Back in my room I spent an hour watching the Food Network and wishing I had a real kitchen. My new house would, once the construction on it was finished. I'd never been much of a cook, but I could always learn. It would be something new to do. And if it turned out I sucked at it, there was always delivery. I'd gained twenty pounds since I'd stopped drinking. To be fair, I'd been damn near skeletal before that. Alcohol had been my primary source of calories and I'd always choose vodka over food when I was too broke to afford both. And even when I'd had money, sometimes I was just too drunk to remember to eat for days at a time. My raging alcoholism had doubled as an incredible weight-loss plan, although not one I could really write a book about and make a million dollars by going on talk shows.

After a while I shut the television off and lay back on the bed, thinking maybe I should take a nap. I felt drained. If I did, though, I'd never sleep tonight, and I really didn't have the option of using alcohol as a sleep aid anymore. I stared at the ceiling for a while, feeling the weight of my Glock still in its shoulder holster. My reverie was interrupted by another text from Dan Evans asking if I was all right. I texted back that I was and he could stop bothering me any time he wanted to. There was little doubt Sarah was keeping him fully apprised of whatever was happening with the copycat case. And probably whatever was happening with me, also.

Around 4:00 pm I took Anita's card out of my pocket and looked at the phone number. I put the card down on the bedside table. I'd said I'd give her a day or two before I turned her down. But part of me didn't want to turn her down anymore. I was bored. I'd been waiting three months for the Laughing Man to reappear so I could finally start hunting him down. He hadn't made a move. There was no telling when he would. To be honest, there was no telling *if* he would. For all I knew he'd been hit by a car while crossing the street. Or he'd had a heart attack. If something had happened to him he could already be in the ground and I'd be left waiting until I joined him.

That left me with nothing to do. I didn't really have any hobbies. I'd started practicing Shotokan karate again after my body had recovered from withdrawal and I could stand up without my legs shaking, but that wasn't something I was going to do every day. Nor did I have much in the way of friends. My life consisted mostly of sitting by myself in a motel room waiting for a lunatic to murder someone so I could start looking for him. How messed up was *that*?

I picked up Anita's card again. She was a great deal sharper than she'd let on; I was sure of that much. That old lady act had probably gotten her pretty far in life. It was intriguing. What was she like when she dropped the act? I wanted to know.

How stupid would I have to be to start investigating a twenty-year-old cold case, though? I hadn't been lying when I'd said it was probably unsolvable. What were the odds I was going to have some kind of breakthrough that had eluded everyone else? Not very damn good. And here I'd just been thinking the Laughing Man could already be dead, and I'd seen him just three months ago. Twenty years was a much longer time. On top of that, I didn't know of a lot of bomb makers that made it to retirement age. The guy had probably blown himself up by now.

But it wasn't as if I had anything better to do.

Eventually I picked up the phone and dialed Anita's number. She answered on the first ring. "This is Nevada James," I said.

"I'm so glad you called, Nevada. How are you?" Her voice was warm and inviting, like she'd just baked an apple pie and wanted to know if I wanted to have my slice with ice cream or a slice of cheese on top. Not that I'd have minded pie. Pie actually sounded pretty good.

"I think we should meet," I said. "Alone this time."

"I'd be happy to," she said. "When would be a good time for you?"

"Tomorrow."

"I can certainly do that," she said. "I'm hosting a luncheon at the La Jolla Country Club at noon. You'd be very welcome to attend as my guest."

"Alone means without other people around," I said. "How about before that?"

"Come by my house for tea? Around ten?"

"That works for me," I said.

She gave me her address, which was to a house in a gated community in Rancho Santa Fe. I didn't expect it would be hard to find. I could just start following BMWs if I couldn't find the neighborhood. "I'll see you then," I said.

"Thank you, dear," she said. She hung up. I stared at my phone for a moment. What the hell had I just gotten myself into?

Chapter 5

The next morning dawned foggy and cool, which was typical for San Diego more days than not. The fog would most likely burn off by noon and the rest of the day would be frustratingly pleasant. I had a Diet Coke and half a bag of chips for breakfast. It was the most important meal of the day, after all.

After a cursory check of the parking lot I got in my Mustang and headed out to I-5, then turned north up the freeway. Rancho Santa Fe was a small community about half an hour north of the city. I'd heard that, demographically speaking, it was one of the wealthiest places in the country, but that really wasn't something I kept track of. I did know that even with the money Alan Davies had paid me, I couldn't have begun to afford a house there. Not that I'd really have wanted one. I wore jeans and t-shirts more often than not and tended to stick out like a sore thumb among more refined company.

A quick check on Google had told me than Anita Collins was an heiress, her great-grandfather having invented cars. Well, not *cars*. It had been some extremely important engine component. The technical part of it hadn't really interested me. Checking her for a criminal background had been easy, and come up negative. The same held true for her husband and every member of their immediate family I could find. There was nothing that made me think they'd had any enemies, either political or personal. People had secrets, of course, but if Anita or her husband had rubbed someone the wrong way badly enough to put their lives in danger, that was something that was going to take a little more effort to dig up.

Anita's neighborhood was in the hills, beyond a gate guarded by a uniformed man in a little booth. The guard looked to be in his fifties, with graying hair and a build that suggested he still worked out. He took in the Mustang and gave me a quick once-over. I expected him to tell me I was probably lost, but before I even had the chance to speak he said, "Good morning, Detective James. Welcome to Playa del Mar. We're happy to have you."

I stared at him. "Good god. Was that a *guess*?"

He hit a switch in the booth and the gate began to open. "I'm not that good," he smiled. "We were told to expect you."

"And you knew what I looked like and what I was driving?"

"I saw you on the news," he admitted. "And I was a cop myself, back in the day. Traffic."

He didn't look familiar to me, but the odds weren't great that I'd have recognized someone from Traffic, anyway. How did you end up here?" I asked. "You write one of the mayor's buddies a ticket?"

"Honestly? This pays a heck of a lot better than being a cop did."

40

That almost seemed hard to believe, until I thought about what I'd made as a cop. It hadn't been a lot, and cops didn't get Christmas bonuses from millionaires. Well, a few probably did, at least until Internal Affairs caught up with them.

There were only eight houses in the neighborhood, all of them sprawling Spanish-style mansions. Anita's wasn't hard to find. I pulled into the driveway, parking next to an immaculate Mercedes. My Mustang looked cheap next to it, but then again, so did I.

I was a bit surprised when Anita answered the door herself shortly after I rang the doorbell. "Good morning, Nevada." She smiled warmly at me.

"I was kind of expecting a butler," I said. "English accent? Overly starched tuxedo?"

"I don't have a butler," she said. "I never really felt the need. It's just me here. Do come in."

Anita wore a sleeved blue cocktail dress today, conservative but still fancy enough she'd probably turn some heads at the event she was going to later. I suspected the conservative aspect of the dress wasn't born as much out of modesty as it was to cover what had happened to her body. I could see more burns near her left wrist where the sleeve ended. They probably went all the way up her arm.

She caught me looking and laughed pleasantly. "I'm afraid I don't wear a lot of swimsuits anymore," she said, tugging the sleeve down a bit. "Let's go sit down. I made a pot of tea. Or...do you prefer coffee? I can put some on if you'd like."

"Tea is fine," I said. I was more interested in watching her kindly grandmother act at this point than I was in enjoying hot beverages. She led me into a sitting room, putting her hand on my arm at one point. The contact suggested both that we were old friends and that she might need the support. Neither of those things were true. She was good at this. I was willing to bet she'd had a lot of practice. I'd seen better liars before, though. Not *much* better, but once you knew what you were looking for, it got easier to spot them.

The sitting room was just off of the main staircase. We sat across from each other on blue couches that had probably cost more than my car. Between us she'd placed a silver tray with a teapot and china cups on a long wooden coffee table. I took a moment to look around; the room was lined with paintings of her family. Her husband had been a handsome man, provided the artist could be trusted not to have taken liberties with his depiction. Adam had been tall, well-built, and had a smile that could have melted ice. Anita's curly-haired son watched me with blue eyes that had been frozen in time for twenty years. What would he be doing now, if he'd lived? With the advantages he'd had in life, he could probably be doing anything. I'd always had a soft spot for children. It had gotten me into a lot of trouble in the past.

Anita poured the tea into two cups and took one for herself. I ignored mine. "I like this room," Anita said. "Sometimes when I sit here I feel as if I'm with my family again." She sighed as if she'd just eaten a fine dessert. "I do so miss them."

"I imagine you do."

She gave me a warm look. "Do you have a family, Nevada?"

"You already know I don't," I said.

Her brow wrinkled a bit as she raised her teacup to her lips. "Did I? I don't recall your saying."

"The thing is," I said, "I'm really good with masks. I've seen a lot of them. Why don't you go ahead and take yours off now?"

Anita sipped her tea, took one small swallow, and then put her cup back down. We looked at each other for a long moment, her radiating the warmth and sincerity that must have dazzled so many, and then it went off like a light switch. Her kind eyes were gone. They were ice now. The contrast was so striking that if I'd left the room a moment earlier and come back in just now I might have asked this woman where her sister Anita went. This was nobody's grandmother. This was a goddess of rage.

"Thank you," she said. "I get so sick of that."

"You're very good," I said. "It's a little scary." Anita didn't look like she wanted to tuck me into bed anymore. She looked like she wanted to murder everyone on Earth. Her voice was different now, too. It was deeper, hard, and edged like a weapon. I realized I'd been off on her age, as well. She was at least ten years younger than I'd thought.

"Nobody wants this," she said, pointing to her face. "Nobody can *handle* this. They want their grandmother from the movies, so I give it to them." She smirked. "What gave me away?"

"Monsters can always see other monsters," I said. "But you knew that. It's why you wanted me."

She pursed her lips. "I might not have put it like that," she said. "I barely remembered who you were before the other night, when I saw you on television. Then I remembered. You're driven. You're a hunter. Going after the Laughing Man nearly drove you insane, but you're still out there doing it. That's what I want."

I glanced around the room. "Bringing me in here to look at pictures of your dead family was a nice touch. Tug at my heartstrings a bit?"

"That wasn't a lie," she said. "I do spend most of my time in this room. Don't ever doubt my devotion to my family." She nodded at a portrait on the far wall. The three of them were pictured standing together on a grassy field near a lake, with sailboats passing by in the background. "They were my entire life, Nevada."

"That much is obvious. You've been sitting on this for twenty years, just...I was going to say *burning* but that sounds really crass. Sorry."

"The word doesn't bother me. It's accurate."

I shook my head. "Jesus. People tell me *I* need therapy. I mean, they're right. I do, but..."

"Listen to your child burn to death and then come talk to me about therapy."

"Fair enough."

"So," she said, "I was going to bring you here and see if you'd be willing to help this," her voice suddenly rose an octave and she was grandma again, "*poor old woman who lost her family find justice after all these years.*" She shook her head and grandma disappeared. "But you've seen through that. I can offer you money, but I know exactly what Alan Davies paid you to find his daughter. You don't need it."

"Wait, you *know* Alan Davies?"

"He's a major donor," she nodded. "Through one of his front companies, of course. He likes to pretend he's part of polite society. I danced with him once at a ball years ago. He was doing the dapper man bit. Everyone thought it was just so *precious*, the handsome young man charming the disfigured old lady." For a moment she looked like she was going to spit on the floor. "Jason told me you were involved in the situation with his missing daughter, so I called him to find out what went on."

"I'll bet he was surprised when he heard your real voice."

"I think *he shit his pants* is closer to the truth."

I had to suppress a laugh. I'd have had to admit I liked this version of Anita a great deal more than the other. This was probably what I'd be like if I lived as long as her, but I knew perfectly well I was going to die long before I ever got old.

"So," she continued. "I can't appeal to you with money. I doubt I can make you feel sorry enough for a poor old lady that you'll help me that way, either."

"I'm wondering what you're left with."

"And I'm wondering if a child's death would do it, because that's what I'm left with."

I leaned back on the couch. "That's a dangerous card to play with me," I said. "The fact that you're old enough to be my mother isn't going to stop me from punching you in the face if you cross the line."

She nodded. "That's your weak point, then." She smiled grimly. "I was fairly certain, but you shouldn't have confirmed it, dear."

45

"Anyone who knows about the last Laughing Man case knows that's my weak spot," I said. "So that's roughly…every adult in San Diego County with a television. It's how Alan Davies got me to take his case. Of course, I was so drunk back then, I'd probably have done it for a case of cheap vodka."

"Then I'm a few months too late for that," she said. "I would have offered you expensive vodka, of course. Once you were done. I wouldn't have wanted you drinking yourself to death before you did the job."

"I was kind of kidding about working for vodka."

"I know, but if that's what it would have taken." She shrugged. "I could appeal to your sense of justice. You were a police officer. My husband and my son were murdered, and their murderer is still walking free."

"If he's still even alive, which isn't a given. It's been twenty years."

"I know he might be dead," Anita said. "But knowing is worth something to me."

I finally took one of the teacups from the table and sipped it. I wasn't a tea person, and while I recognized from the smell that this one was supposed to taste like citrus, it tasted more like someone had managed to screw up boiling water to me. "Tell me," I said. "What would you have me do if I found him?"

She rubbed at the scar on her face. "What if I said I wanted you to bring him here to me and then walk away?"

"I'd say to forget about it. I'm not going to be your executioner."

"Nevada, tell me something. When you catch up with the

Laughing Man, are you planning to arrest him?"

"I think you know I'm not."

She nodded. "Then why should justice be any different for me?"

I thought it over. "You know, I don't have a great answer for that. A long time ago I'd have said we need to believe in the system, but the truth is I don't believe in it anymore. Or maybe I just don't care about the system. When I find the Laughing Man I'm going to kill him. I'm going to do it as slowly as I possibly can. I'm going to make it hurt. But that doesn't mean I'll let you do the same thing. I guess that makes me a hypocrite, but that's just how it's going to have to be."

Anita considered her tea. "Very well. Will you help me, though?"

"Say you'll be satisfied with the system. Arrest and trial."

She looked me in the eyes. "Arrest and trial."

I held her stare for a moment, not sure if she was lying to me or not. Even if she was, she was never going to have a chance to be alone in a room with whoever killed her family. If she was crafty enough, she might be able to have someone killed in prison, but that was tricky, and one word about it from me to Corrections would put the guy in solitary confinement where he'd be untouchable.

"I'll think about it," I said. "I'm not saying yes or no yet. But I'll think about it."

Anita sighed. "I've been waiting long enough not to be in a rush. But I do hope you'll think about it quickly. Time is a factor, if only in the sense that once the Laughing Man kills again, I know you're not going to be taking any new cases."

"Taking cases? Is that what I'm doing now?"

"Isn't it? First for Alan Davies, and now hopefully for me?"

"I don't have a license for this sort of thing, and after my stay in the psych ward I couldn't get one even if I wanted it. It doesn't really matter, though. There isn't a law against going around asking people questions."

"Would you care if there were?"

"No." I sipped the tea, trying to pick up the citrus in it this time. If I concentrated, it tasted like hot water that had been sitting near an orange for a while. "Tell me this. Who do you think did it?"

"I was convinced it was the Unabomber, or a Unabomber copycat, but the FBI said there weren't any known copycats. Now, I just don't know."

"Was your husband's research public? Was it something I could have read about on the Internet." I paused. "*Was* there Internet in 1993?"

"It was different then. Most of the world was still on dial-up bulletin boards. But no, my husband's work was known mostly in the academic community. It wasn't secret, but it would hardly have been accessible to the general public."

"Did you or he have enemies? Tell me now, because I'll just find out anyway and you'll never hear from me again."

"My husband was harmless, Nevada. He was a scientist. He..." her eyes took on a faraway look I knew she wasn't faking. "He was a simple man. Brilliant, but simple. He thought he was going to build computers that would change the world. He believed technology would end famine, poverty, war..." She smiled wistfully. "He used to get so excited about it. I know he was probably naïve, but that's who he was. And he never made an enemy in his life."

"What about you? You've got a lot of money. Money usually comes with problems."

"It's my family's money, and if my great-grandfather screwed anyone over to get it, it happened generations ago. We've been out of the business for decades. I hardly even know what a car engine looks like."

"Any affairs?"

She smirked. "I won't take offense that you asked. No. Not on my part, anyway, and I'd be shocked if Adam had."

"So you don't have a single suspect?"

"No."

I scratched my head. "Okay, what about who gained financially? Artificial intelligence has to be profitable."

"And someday it might have been, but I've had Adam's work reviewed by people who are much smarter on the subject than I am. Adam was a visionary, but nothing he was building actually *worked*. Some of it might have, someday, but the field was still in its infancy. There was nothing in what he had done to steal. Nobody ran off and started a company with anything he did."

"Well, shit," I said.

"I know," Anita said. "I've been at this for a while, Nevada."

I'd have had to admit I was intrigued. And I had very little else to do with my time. It wouldn't kill me to look at the old case files. At the most all I was going to lose was a day or two

I'd just have spent watching bad television in my motel room.

I stood up. "I'm going to go," I said. "I'll call you in a few hours. I want to think about a few things before I make a decision. Will you be reachable after your brunch, or whatever the hell you're doing?"

"Call whenever you like, Nevada. I'll drop everything for you." She stood up and shook my hand. "Regardless of your decision, I'd like to thank you. It's been a while since I could be myself in front of other people." She scrunched up her face around the eyes and a set of wrinkles appeared, adding ten years to her appearance. The grandmother was back. "I *do* hope you'll be discreet, dear," she said, using the singsong voice again.

"You'll have to teach me how to do that someday," I said. "My mask has never been as good as yours."

Chapter 6

I was already pretty sure I was going to take the case, but I was hesitant to just jump into it without talking to someone I trusted first. My list of trusted people was fairly small. You could count them on one hand, and you only needed two fingers. Three, if you counted Sarah Winters, and I wasn't sure I did. I liked her, and I had no reason to think she'd ever betray me, but I was also a paranoid and possibly delusional alcoholic. Trust wasn't something that came easily to me.

The gate leading back to the main street had a motion sensor that made it open automatically for anyone who was leaving, but I stopped at the guard booth anyway. The same guy I'd talked to before was still in there. "What do you think of Anita?" I asked him.

"She's the sweetest lady," he said. "We all just love her."

"Oh, yeah?"

"She brings cookies and lemonade out here on the hot days," he nodded. "Always asks about the kids. Not like some

51

of them in there, who drive by like they don't even see us. She's good people."

"Thanks," I said, putting the car into gear. He may have made a good security guard, but he'd never have been a good detective.

I stopped at a fast food drive-through on the way back to San Diego and ate in the car. I really wanted to talk to someone, but I wasn't sure who to call. Dan Evans was probably still in Santa Fe, and the first thing he was going to say to me was "come back to work." As if that were really an option. Even if I was willing to go back to a life of rules and regulations, being a police officer required a certain amount of psychological stability I didn't have. The other option was...I took my phone out of my pocket and dialed.

Molly Malone answered on the third ring. "Hey."

"Hey. You busy?"

"I've got a class at 2:00, but I'm free after that. You okay?"

"Yeah," I said. "I just want to run something by you. It's not urgent."

"Why don't you come by after?"

"That works."

"See you then."

Molly Malone had been a well-known therapist with several successful books to her credit. She'd taken some of her book money and opened a karate dojo in Pacific Beach several years ago. I'd trained there when I'd been a cop; not having the advantage of physical size or muscle in a job where I could easily find myself up against violent killers, I'd wanted to make sure my fighting skills were top notch. I'd earned a black belt before I made detective.

After the Laughing Man, and after I'd been in the psych ward, Molly had tried taking a turn as my therapist, if only because she knew I wasn't going to talk to anyone else. That hadn't gone well. A long time ago, while I'd been in a drunken rage, I'd told her I never wanted to see her again. We'd only been back in touch for a few months, but I was glad to have her in my life. This time it was as friends only; she'd said she couldn't fill both roles for me. She'd recommended half a dozen other therapists for me to see since we'd started talking again, but I had yet to actually visit one of them.

Pacific Beach was a small community on the western side of San Diego that catered to surfers, hipsters, and people who liked both nightclubs and overpriced alcohol. I was none of those things. Even when I'd been drinking, I only did it alone. My version of nightlife when I'd been a cop consisted of picking through crime scenes, then going home to down enough vodka to knock me out. After a while it had been the only way I could go to sleep.

I got into Pacific Beach a little before 3:00. It was early enough that traffic was still light; Pacific Beach really only had one major thoroughfare that went in and out of the neighborhood, and it would be clogged well before rush hour hit. Coffee shops, trendy restaurants, and bars lined both sides of the street, as did surfer dudes and homeless people. When it got dark the surfers would leave and the hipsters would arrive. The homeless and the crazies never left. I saw a raggedy man arguing with a mailbox, and nearer Molly's dojo a guy who could have passed for an otherwise normal professional in his thirties was having an animated discussion with a cat. I wondered what *his* problem was. Drugs or alcohol, probably. Had I ever argued with a cat when I'd been drinking? Probably. That or worse.

Molly's dojo was at the end of a strip mall near the beach. I parked out front and went inside. Molly was easy to spot. She was exactly five feet tall and probably weighed a hundred pounds soaking wet, but sometimes big surprises came in small packages. Even when I'd been in my best shape, Molly had been able to wipe the floor with me on the mat. One of these days, when I was back in top form, we were going to have to try that again. In the meantime, though, I tried to get in here once or twice a week to work out and build my body back up from the physical wreck it had become during my drinking days.

Molly was still in her *gi*. She trotted over and hugged me as soon as she saw me. Molly was also a hugger. I needed to introduce her to Sarah. Maybe they could start a hugging club. "You want to spar?" she asked me.

"Nah," I said. "Not today. You got time to go get coffee?"

"Sure. Let's go across the street. The new place finally opened."

The new place turned out to be a Starbucks, which made at least three different Starbucks within walking distance of the dojo. I wondered how many people needed to want coffee at the same time in order for that to be profitable, but overexpansion didn't seem to be hurting their stock price. "So what's going on?" Molly asked once we'd sat down.

The triple espresso I'd ordered was still too hot to chug, which was how I liked to drink it. I swirled the liquid around in the cup once. "You know I saw a dude arguing with a cat on the way in here? What do you think that was about?"

"I think you're in Pacific Beach, Nevada. It's a slow day if that's the only weird thing you saw. Now stop avoiding the question and tell me what's going on." She gave me a skeptical look. "If you're drinking again you're putting on a hell of a sober act right now."

"No. I'm clean and sober."

"How's that working out for you?"

"I hate it worse than cancer."

Molly shook her head. "Well, that seems kind of excessive. I know it's not easy, but you look a lot better than you did three months ago. I thought you were on death's door. You still going to A.A.?"

"Now and again, but booze isn't why I wanted to talk to you. There's this job..."

She frowned. "The Laughing Man copycat thing? I saw it on the news."

"No, not that. I mean, they actually did call me in to look at the crime scene, and one of the detectives wanted to ask me some questions about it, but I'm not involved other than that."

"Good. What's the job, then?"

I broke down the Anita Collins situation for her. It only took a few minutes. She listened without interrupting, sipping her vanilla chai intermittently until I was done. Then she thought it over and I wondered what her vanilla chai tasted like. I'd never had one, but from where I was sitting it smelled like Christmas.

Finally she broke her silence. "That woman sounds

damaged beyond repair."

"I wasn't trying to refer her to you," I said. "I get it, though. She's been sitting on this for twenty years. If I lived to be her age, I'd probably wind up the same way."

"You think you won't live that long, Nevada?"

"I know I won't live that long." Molly frowned at me. "That's not depression speaking. With the damage I've done to my body, there's just no chance. And that's assuming the Laughing Man doesn't kill me before I can kill him." I studied the expression on her face. "If you were frowning any harder I might turn to stone."

She looked away. "Damn it, Nevada," she said.

"Leave it. What's done is done."

"Well, at some point I'm going to drag you in to see an internist, but that's not what you came here for. You want to know if you should look for the killer."

"Yeah."

Molly sighed. "You know, why is it every time we have a conversation it's never about...I don't know. Politics, or the last book we read, or even *men*, for god's sake?"

"Did you start dating men without telling me?"

"No, but that wasn't the point and you know it. You come by and we spar, which is good. You need to get out of the house and be active again. But your life is so colossally fucked up, Nevada..."

"You mean everyone doesn't have a serial killer obsessed with them? I just assumed..."

She jabbed a finger at me. "See? That right there! Any rational person would be going out of their damn mind about that, but you just make jokes. You act like he's your annoying ex-boyfriend holding up a boom box outside your window, trying to get back together with you. You need to get your mind right."

"Remember how when we talk now it's as friends, and not as therapist and patient?"

"That *was* me talking as your friend. If I was your therapist I'd call the police."

My espresso was finally cool enough to drink. I downed it in one swallow, grimacing like I'd done a shot of whiskey. "Just tell me what you think."

"I think I'm about to tear my damn hair out talking to you."

"We'll stop at the salon after."

She made a noise that sounded suspiciously like *harrumph*, if that was a noise people actually made. "Take the job. Go look for the bomber. You won't find him, but who cares?"

"Really?" I asked.

"Well, what else are you going to do? Sit around your motel room and wait for the Laughing Man to send you flowers again? That sounds miserable."

"I don't know," I said. "It's given me a lot of time to catch up on daytime television. I saw an episode of Maury Povich the other day. You know Maury?" She stared daggers at me. "See, there was this woman who had a baby, and this guy was like, 'That's not *my* baby,' but then Maury whipped out this *lie detector*..."

"Nevada…"

"Don't tell me you've seen that one? I don't want to ruin it for you, but it actually *was* his baby…"

She stood up. "That's it. Let's go."

"Where?"

"If you've got time to sit here and make jokes, then you've got time to work out. Come on. I'm going to kick your ass."

Chapter 7

Half an hour later I was lying on my back on a padded mat in Molly's dojo looking up at the light fixtures overhead. One of these days I'd be able to breathe again. Maybe I'd even get really ambitious and try standing up.

Molly had been exaggerating, of course. If she'd really wanted to hurt me, I'd probably be dead. But she hadn't minded smacking me around her dojo like a cat playing with an overweight, asthmatic mouse. "Are you even sweating?" I asked her.

She reached out a hand and helped me up. "No. You're getting stronger, though. Maybe I'll sweat next time."

"I guess I'm getting better, then" I said. "I still feel like a kid when I fight you."

Molly bowed. I bowed back. "You're at about 40% of where you used to be," she said.

"That's *it?*"

"Well, no," she said. "I just didn't want you to feel bad. It's more like 30%. Any of my faster brown belts could take you."

"Oh." I wiped the sweat off my forehead with my sleeve. "At least I'm not puking every time I exercise anymore."

"There you go," she said. "Okay, I've got another class coming up. You want to stick around, or are you going to take off?"

"I'm going to take off. I think I deserve a pizza after this."

She gave me a long look. "You be careful out there, Nevada. Look into the case, see what you think, but don't take any chances. It's probably not going to go anywhere after twenty years, but if things get weird or it starts screwing with your head, just walk away."

"I doubt anything is going to get weird."

"It's you we're talking about, so I'm pretty sure *something* is going to get weird."

She gave me another hug and went to get ready for her class. I took a shower in the locker room and put my street clothes back on. I had my own locker and *gi* here, and Molly still let me wear my black belt even though I really wasn't at that level anymore. I'd get there. It was just going to take time. Three months ago I'd come in here stinking of vodka and she'd destroyed me like it was nothing. At least this time it had looked like she'd needed to pay attention while she kicked my ass.

I hit rush hour traffic on the way out of Pacific Beach, but it wasn't as if I was in a hurry to get anywhere. It gave me time to think things over. Anita's case was interesting, if way outside my area of expertise. I'd been a homicide detective, and while what had happened to her family certainly qualified as murder, most people picked guns or knives as their weapons of choice. Bombs were a lot more unusual, if for no better reason than they weren't all that easy to make. I wondered if I should go pick up a chemistry textbook. I could also do a Google search for "how to make bombs and kill people," but that might get me a visit from Homeland Security. Probably not, but there was no point in getting myself a spot on the no-fly list.

Back at the motel I ordered a sausage and mushroom pizza for delivery and spent half an hour looking at one of my early Laughing Man case files. His first kill, at least the first we knew about, had been a high society woman in her forties. Her body had been found on a patio chair next to a swimming pool with a Mai Tai next to her. It had been the first time anyone had seen the Laughing Man's bloody smile. Nobody knew what to make of it at the time. The only thing I'd been sure of back then was that this was something new. Murders that took place out of anger or jealousy were old hat to me by then. I'd even worked a couple serial killer cases, but those had been simple by comparison. The Laughing Man was something unique.

He'd come to feel the same way about me, eventually. Three years ago he'd had me dead to rights, had beaten me within an inch of my life, and then, at the moment we both knew he should kill me, he'd turned and walked away. And then he went dark. The cops hadn't understood why. How was it that his compulsions didn't *make* him kill again?

The answer was simple. Because it wasn't about compulsion for him. It was a game. If he killed me, he'd have had nobody left to play with. Sitting at a chessboard by yourself isn't any fun.

Now I was back on my feet, but he hadn't started the game

yet. It's amazing how bored you can get when you're ready to play, but the other player refuses to take his seat at the table.

My pizza came and I ate two slices, then put the rest in the tiny motel refrigerator. The rest of it would be tomorrow's breakfast, or maybe a midnight snack if I woke up and was hungry. I'd tried placating my urge to drink with junk food, with mixed results. On one hand, I didn't get drunk. On the other, it was getting hard to remember the last time I'd seen a real vegetable.

I was watching some terrible police drama on television when there was a knock at the door. I took my Glock out of its holster and pointed it at the peephole. "Who is it?" I called.

"Open the door, Nevada," Dan Evans said. His deep voice sounded like an avalanche. Well, I'd never been in an avalanche, so that was a guess. I probably wasn't far off, though.

I put the gun down on the bed and went to open the door. Dan stood there, a suitcase in one hand. He looked like he'd missed a day of shaving. Behind him I could see a taxi pulling out of the motel parking lot. "Jesus," I said. "Did you come here straight from the airport?"

"It's on the way home," he said. "You going to invite me in?"

I moved away from the door and shut it once he was inside. Dan was a bear of a man, too tall and too wide for any of the clothes he bought, but he'd never yet let me take him shopping. Not that I knew a great deal about men's fashion, or fashion at all for that matter, but at least I could find the Big & Tall section in a department store.

Dan put his suitcase down and stood with his hands on his hips, his eyes lingering for a second on the Glock on my bed, before surveying the rest of the room. Without a word he went to the bathroom, flipped the light on, and looked inside.

"You want to check the drawers, too?" I asked. "That's where I keep the booze." I hoped he wouldn't pick up that my sarcasm was a bluff and decide to look in there for himself. I didn't want to explain my nightly ritual to him. He'd never understand it.

He eyed the dresser but didn't look inside. "You can't blame me for being concerned."

"I don't blame you," I said. "I did tell you I'm fine, though."

"You said the same thing five minutes before you had your first seizure."

He'd told me I'd said that before, but I couldn't remember it. I'd quit drinking cold turkey when I finally stopped. That had been a serious mistake. It turned out *delirium tremens* was a very real thing, and I'd spent two nightmarish days in the hospital while my body demonstrated that to me. "Fair enough," I said.

He looked at the Glock again. "You know something funny, Nevada? That looks like a Glock, and I can't seem to remember giving you a Glock."

"You didn't. The Glock fits my hand better. The .45 you gave me is in the nightstand."

"You don't like the .45?"

"I never said I didn't like it, but it's huge. You might as well have gotten me a shotgun."

"You're getting a shotgun when you move into your house," he said.

"Funny man."

"You think I was kidding?" he asked. He picked up the Glock and looked it over. "This one of the new 19's?"

"Yeah."

"Is it legal for you to have it?"

"Possession is nine tenths of the law."

Dan looked up at me. "Do I even want to know where you got this thing?"

"No."

He sighed and put it back down, then sat on the bed next to it. "We should talk."

I took one of the motel chairs near the window. "Dan, you know I love you, but you are getting very close to pissing me off with this watchdog shit."

He looked at me for a long moment, probably trying to size me up. "Sarah told me she had you come out to the crime scene."

"Yeah. You mad about that? It was a possible Laughing Man case, and I'm more or less the expert on those. It was the right call."

"That much I know."

"Then what? You thought I'd see the dead guy's face and start having flashbacks? I don't have PTSD."

"You absolutely have PTSD," Dan said. "You have so much PTSD they should name a new variety of it for you."

I shrugged. The point wasn't worth arguing, and he was probably right, anyway. "Well, I didn't have any flashbacks. I don't wake up in cold sweats. I have been having these recurring nightmares, though…"

Dan leaned forward. "About him?"

"No," I said. "I keep dreaming that California gets invaded by these robot people from another dimension and I have to lead a resistance movement to fight them. And I make friends with a werewolf." I shook my head. "I can't imagine what it means."

"For god's sake," Dan sighed. "Can't you be serious for five seconds?"

"Nope."

"Of course not," he said. "Well, at least you're sober."

"I am. Want to ask me how much I'm enjoying it?"

"I don't care how much you're enjoying it."

I kind of wanted to get on Dan's case for barging in here this way, but the truth was I deserved it. I'd put him through a lot. Dan was one of the only people that had never given up on me, and I was a person who actually deserved to have been given up on.

"Anyway," he said, "I didn't really think you were drinking."

"Then what were you so worried about? Oh, of course. You were afraid you'd forget to give me the souvenir you brought me from Santa Fe." I looked at his suitcase. "You are going to tell me there's a souvenir in there, right? Is it a t-shirt?"

"No."

"Is it a mug?"

"I didn't get you a souvenir, Nevada."

I clucked my tongue at him. "It's like you don't care about me anymore," I said. "If I went to Santa Fe, I'd get you a souvenir."

"No, you wouldn't. Anyway, Sarah told me you looked over the crime scene."

"Of course I looked over the crime scene. She didn't ask me over there to perform musical theater with them."

He ignored my clever remark. "She said you told them it wasn't the Laughing Man."

"It wasn't," I said. "She knew it, too. I think she just wanted me to confirm it before she made the call."

"And when she called me afterward, she was worried about you. She said you were completely emotionless about it. Like you didn't give a shit. You looked at a dead body and called it *trash*."

I tried to resist the urge to roll my eyes. "Okay, that wasn't my best choice of words ever."

"She said you were like a robot."

"Now that's just *mean*," I pouted. "I don't know how I'm going to get to sleep tonight after hearing that."

"Damn it, Nevada, you know what I'm getting at." He leaned forward on the bed and interlaced his fingers. "Human beings *react* to that kind of thing."

I stood up. "I'm getting a Diet Coke," I said. "You want a

Diet Coke?"

"Did you hear anything I just said?"

"Yeah, but I'm thirsty. Do you want the soda or not?"

He shrugged. "Sure."

I went to the refrigerator and took two cans out, handing him one as I went back to my chair. Mine I popped open and raised like I was toasting him, then took a drink. "I don't know what you want to hear," I said after a minute. "No, that's not true. I do know what you want to hear. You want to hear that I was affected by it."

He opened his own can and took a sip. "I do want to hear that, yeah."

"Too bad," I said. "I wasn't. I don't have that in me anymore, Dan. Don't get me wrong. I know I *should*. I'm perfectly aware that I've lost some part of me I used to have. Well, that's just too bad. It's just spilt milk."

He nearly choked on his soda. "It's *spilt milk*? That may be the worst analogy you've ever made."

"Well, technically it's an idiom, but I don't think it quite worked. It's water under the bridge? No..."

"We're having a serious conversation, Nevada. Remember?"

"I think you're the one having a serious conversation," I said. "I'm still worried about those robots from my dream."

He ignored that. "I remember you were upset when you broke that guy's neck. The one Emerson sent over to waste you. You're telling me you went from that to this in three months?"

"No," I said, "but I was drunk then. And *I* was the one who killed him, and I didn't mean to do it. He was just some stooge I hit too hard. It's not the same thing as seeing some dead guy in an alley." Dan grunted. "Give me a break," I said. "Do Sarah and that guy Ellis come cry on your shoulder every time they catch a homicide?"

"No."

"Would they be good detectives if they did?"

"No, but everyone deals with it differently. Sarah's been in therapy for five years and Brad...he was for a while, anyway. He was in a shoot a while back and couldn't clear his psych evaluation after, so I made him do some couch time until he could."

I put my soda down. "Sarah's in therapy?"

He smirked. "Oh, look at you now. Are you actually concerned with another person's welfare?"

"Don't be a dick," I said, just a little more coldly than I meant to.

"I wasn't. It's nice to see you have an emotion. Yeah, Sarah's in therapy. I encourage my people to talk to a professional whether they think they need to or not. You can't take all that shit home. If I'd made you go when you worked for me maybe you wouldn't have lost your shit the way you did."

"I'd have liked to see you try to 'make me' do anything," I said. "That would have been fun."

He drank his soda. "I really don't know what I expected this conversation to sound like," he said, "but this wasn't it."

68

"Me neither," I said. "This is the longest we've talked in a while without you offering me my badge back."

"It's in my desk at the office. You want me to go get it?"

"No."

"It would be good for you," he said. "At least you wouldn't be sitting around here all day."

For a moment I thought about telling him about my conversation with Anita Collins, but I decided against it. He'd probably just find a reason to lecture me. "I'm fine," I said. "I could never go back, anyway. Somehow I think I'd fail the background check now."

He gave me a contemplative look. "There are ways."

"You going to strong-arm someone?" I asked. "Blackmail the Chief if he says no?"

"The Chief would take you back."

"The Chief *hates* me," I said.

"Oh, he does hate you, Nevada. He hates you worse than Hitler. But you close cases. He likes *that*. With the media attention this copycat thing is getting, I could swear you in tonight and he'd probably come in to give us medals at the same time."

He was exaggerating about the medals, probably, but I also knew he was serious about the job. I was a special case. If I'd wanted it, they'd find a way to make it work. A tiny part of me did want it. The rational part of me knew it would be a huge mistake.

"No," I said. He opened his mouth and I held up a hand. "Don't tell me to think about it. I have thought about it. I'll probably think about it more. If I change my mind, I'll let you know."

He nodded. "Fine. I guess I'll have to take that, for now. But swearing you in isn't the only way we could do it. We could probably appoint you as a consultant."

"A consultant? What the fuck is that, Dan?"

"I don't know, all right? Damn it, Nevada, I just want you out of this room."

"I've got an interview at McDonald's coming up," I said. "I don't have a ton of experience with food, but I hear they're not all that picky…"

"Shut up, Nevada."

He finished his soda and belched under his breath. "One other thing."

"Okay, Columbo."

He ignored that. "Why did you tell Sarah not to investigate the copycat?"

"I didn't say that," I said. "I said not to bother. It's not the same thing. And you know exactly why I said it. She already told you."

"Yeah, I know what she said."

"You thinking I've gone mental?"

"I already know you've gone mental," he said. "I was just wondering if you're going to go look for this guy yourself, and then sit on him until the Laughing Man shows up to kill him."

I raised my eyebrows as if that had never occurred to me. "That's not a bad idea," I said. "Hey, can you get me a copy of the case file? I just want it for no reason."

"Nevada…"

"I was kidding," I said. "I'm not looking for him. I'm not going to say I never thought about it, but I'm not looking."

"Why not?"

"Because say I did find him. You think I'm going to sit by while he kills someone else, just because I'm hoping the Laughing Man is going to show up for me to shoot? I'm mental, but I'm not *that* mental." I thought about that. "You know, that might not have been my answer three months ago. See? I'm making progress!"

Dan stood up. "Go fuck yourself, Nevada," he said.

"Love you, too."

"You have my number," he said. "Call me if you need to. I'll check in on you in a few days."

"What for?"

"Because I care about you, you stupid shit." He took his phone out of his jacket and called for a cab. "Take care of yourself, all right?"

"You, too."

"Try not to get in any trouble."

"You know me," I said. "What could possibly happen?"

He glanced at the Glock sitting on my bed. "Knowing you? Almost anything."

Chapter 8

An hour after Dan left I took the vodka out of the dresser and poured half an inch into a cup. I sat with it while I watched part of a talk show, then poured it down the drain. I wondered if the need to do that was ever going to go away. It wouldn't be the end of the world if it didn't. It probably would be if I ever drank it. If I went down that hole again there wasn't much chance I was ever coming back.

In the morning I called Anita at the number she'd given me. "Hello?" she answered in her grandmother voice.

"I'll take the job," I said.

"I'm glad to hear it," she said. The grandmother voice was gone. "Let's talk about money."

"We don't need to talk about money," I said. "I doubt this is going to go anywhere. If I'm wrong about that, you can pay me whatever you think it's worth. Alan Davies gave me a small fortune to find his daughter. I'm not going to need money for a long time."

"When you find the murderer, I'm sure you won't have any complaints about your compensation," she said. "I'll make sure you never need money again."

There was more than one way to take that, but somehow I doubted Anita meant it in the sense that I wouldn't need money because she'd have me killed. Maybe that meant my paranoia was improving. "I really do doubt I'm going to come up with anything," I said. "I'm going to start digging, though. You sure there's nothing you need to tell me before I start? If I'm going to uncover embezzlement or affairs or something like that, you may as well tell me now."

"Nothing like that. My husband was as upstanding and true a man as you could ever want to meet."

I tried not to snicker. That had been more than a little over the top. Then again, it had sounded like she'd meant it. "Yeah, great. Look, I don't *care*, all right? Unless you were running a child slavery ring or something, I'm not going to judge you. But if I find out you've lied to me, I'm going to be pretty pissed about it. People say I'm not much fun when I'm pissed."

"I have no trouble believing that," Anita said.

"All right. I'm going to get in touch with Jason London and tell him I want the case file. I'd rather nobody else found out I was looking at this; it might cause some friction with the SDPD." I paused. "What's your connection to Jason, anyway? He said you were a friend, but I don't really see you two hanging out in the same social circles."

"No, we don't. One of my foundations provides supplemental healthcare costs for police officers and firefighters."

"And?"

"I paid for his rehab."

I frowned. "I'd think the SDPD's insurance would cover rehab."

"It doesn't cover a month at Passages."

I knew the name. Passages was a rehab facility in Malibu that was known for treating celebrities. I had no idea what it cost, but it was probably more than Jason made in a year. "Okay," I said. "I guess I can see that. Anyway, I'll be in touch."

"Thank you, Nevada. I appreciate this more than you'll ever know."

I hung up. She'd never gone back to using her singsong voice with me. That had been wise. I wondered how many people she let through that wall.

I was hungry and cold pizza for breakfast didn't sound appealing. I decided to text Jason first, though. *Need case file for Collins. Going to take a look.* He replied two minutes later. *Already have it ready. Where to meet?* I didn't feel like having him over to my motel room, so I sent back the name of a diner I knew near Old Town and went to the window for my usual routine of looking for anything suspicious in the parking lot. As was also the usual, nothing stood out. If the Laughing Man was watching me, he was doing it from a distance. Then again, he probably knew my routines better than I did. They never varied much. It wasn't as if I'd taken Alan Davies's money and started a life of jet-setting around the globe.

The diner was about half full when I went inside. I ordered an omelet and hash browns and sipped a Diet Coke while I waited. Jason walked in just as the food was coming to the table. He was wearing aviator sunglasses with a Tommy Bahama shirt and shorts. "You look like a drug dealer," I said when he got to the table.

"I'm buying half a ton of weed later," he said, sitting down. "Some people appreciate the look."

"You look like you're in an action movie from the 90's. Bruce Willis is going to come in here and mess up your shit."

"It's okay. I have a ninja army standing by."

For a moment I was shocked, then I laughed. "You aren't usually funny," I said.

He shrugged. "I'm not usually in this good a mood. I appreciate you helping Anita like this."

"Helping people is what I do," I said. "I'm like..." I thought it over but couldn't come up with anything clever, "somebody who is always helping. Damn. That one got away from me."

"Nobody's perfect."

I looked him over. "So where are the files?"

"In my trunk." The waiter came by and Jason ordered two soft-boiled eggs and coffee.

"Why are they in the trunk?" I asked. "I was expecting you to give me a thumb drive."

He shook his head. "Nothing that old has been digitized. You're getting three dusty boxes. That's it."

I sighed. "Why can't anything be easy?"

Jason's food came and he tucked into his soft-boiled eggs.

"I meant it before. It's nice of you to help Anita."

"It'll come to nothing, I'm sure. Have you looked at the files?"

"Yeah, but it's not my field. What do I know about bomb analysis? There were never any serious suspects. They interviewed a couple aging hippies that were involved in the anti-war scene."

"Desert Storm? Did that even count as a war?"

"No, the Vietnam War. You've heard of it?"

"Yeah, that's the one that had to do with the impressment of sailors."

Jason stared at me. "What?"

"Forget it. It was a War of 1812 joke. Actually, it was probably the *only* War of 1812 joke. Of course I've heard of Vietnam. Why were they interviewing old hippies?"

He shrugged. "The hippies had their share of radicals. One of them had been part of a group that was suspected of putting a bomb under a police car in 1968. They were fighting the power, or the pigs, or whatever people said back then."

"I think they were worried about 'the man' always getting them down."

"That sounds about right."

"You like any of them for it?"

"No. It's a pretty big stretch to go from anti-war to blowing up a guy that wanted to make smart computers. I always figured it was a jealous lover, but Anita says neither of them had a lover, and I believe her."

"What's your take on Anita?"

Jason sipped his coffee. "She's a sweet old lady. Means the world to me. I assume you know she helped me out?"

"Yeah." So Jason hadn't seen through her mask, either. The woman was good. I wondered if she'd fronted the rehab costs through her foundation because she wanted a cop to owe her a favor. That actually seemed pretty likely. "What about the bomb?"

"Pretty standard pipe bomb. You could get the instructions to make one off the Internet."

"Or whatever passed for the Internet in 1993, I guess."

"Yeah. I think I had CompuServe back then. You could probably find stuff like that in the forums."

"I remember *The Anarchist's Cookbook*," I said. "I think that was just hype, though, and not anything you could actually use." I shrugged. "I have no idea, really. I'll probably have to do some research."

"Or go ask someone who makes bombs."

I could tell from his smirk that he'd been joking, but that wasn't a bad idea. I knew more than a few criminals, some in prison, and some not. A few of them owed me.

I put a $20 bill on the table when Jason was finished eating and we went to his car, where we transferred three file boxes from his trunk to mine. They were dustier than I expected. "Somehow I doubt anyone's looked at these in the last year," I said.

"Besides me, probably not. And I didn't spend a lot of time with them."

I slammed my trunk shut. "Anything else you can think to tell me?"

"Well, I haven't seen you at a meeting in a while." He gave me a concerned look. "Are you avoiding us for a reason?"

"No," I said. "I've just been really busy with not going."

"People worry about you."

I shook my head. "Jason, honestly, I don't need to hear this. I didn't say I'm done with it, but I'm never going to be one of those people who goes to A.A. every day. I don't need it to stay clean. I have things to do besides talk about the steps and the higher power and...whatever else. Tell everyone I said 'hi' if that makes them feel better."

"I will. I just think people would rather hear it from you."

"Then they're going to have to wait," I said. "I have a case to work."

Chapter 9

I'd told Jason I had a case to work mostly because I wanted him to shut up, but I found that saying it felt good. I finally had something to do. It was almost like having a real job again. That was new. Actually, having a job while I was sober was new. I'd been half in the bag while I'd been out looking for Alan Davies's daughter. It was a miracle I'd managed to find her. Well, it had been either a miracle or dumb luck. Probably the latter.

Once I got back to my motel I transferred the file boxes from the truck to my bed, then sat down and watched two episodes of a Law & Order marathon. I didn't care for the show, but it beat Maury Povich or one of those court shows where a television judge yelled at a couple idiots who were fighting over the price of a bad haircut or something equally inane. I'd have been a terrible television judge. It would have been too tempting to start smacking people around with the gavel. Then again, doing that might have turned it into the highest-rated show on television.

After deciding I'd procrastinated long enough, I opened the first box of files and started going through them. The first ones I read were specific to the bomb itself. From the fragments that had been recovered, the investigators had determined that it had been constructed from a piece of steel pipe about five inches long and one inch in diameter. It had been triggered by a tripwire. Photos of the burned-out car showed it had been a total loss. It was difficult to believe anyone had made it out of that pile of twisted metal alive, but Anita had.

I looked over a list of the bomb's components. Gunpowder had been the primary explosive agent. I knew next to nothing about pipe bombs, and I'd never have thought something that small could be so powerful. I'd figured it would have made a loud bang, and maybe you'd lose a finger if you were holding it, like an overly large firecracker.

A curious notation included hydrogen peroxide among the bomb's ingredients, but someone had put a question mark next to it. A chemical formula had been circled, but the string of H's and O's didn't mean much to me. Hydrogen peroxide didn't make any sense, though. It was a liquid, and it certainly didn't explode. My parents had used it to clean cuts and scrapes I'd gotten roughhousing with other kids when I'd been younger. How could it possibly have been mixed with gunpowder? That had to be a mistake.

Full-color photos of Anita's naked body had been taken to catalog her injuries. Looking at them was both awkward and horrifying. I wasn't surprised to see that burns ran down the entire left side of her body, but she'd been a lot worse than singed. In places her skin had been charred black; third-degree burns that made her look like she'd been put together from pieces of dead flesh like Frankenstein's monster. Her face had looked a great deal worse then, but plastic surgery and time had obviously helped. There wouldn't have been much all the surgeons in the world could have done for her torso and leg, though. I wondered how long it had taken her to heal. She must have been in the hospital for months.

I went to my refrigerator to get a Diet Coke. The smell of leftover pizza wafted out when I opened the door, making me instantly nauseous. There was very little chance I was going to eat it now. After a moment's deliberation over the guilt I'd feel about it, I took the box outside and threw it in the dumpster. I hated wasting food, but I didn't want to smell it, or anything else, for a while.

A photocopy of the warning note Adam Collins had been sent was in the files. It was simple enough, written in all capitals and looking as if it had come off an early laser printer. NO SMART COMPUTERS, it read. STOP NOW OR ELSE. That suggested the bomber had had an agenda, but it could also be an attempt at misdirection. The "or else" sounded juvenile to me, or maybe it was just someone who wasn't used to writing threatening notes. It wasn't like that was something people did every day.

The note had been found on the windshield of the car that had been bombed a month before the attack. That didn't suggest a crime of passion. Whoever had sent it, provided it *was* the bomber, had given Collins time to change his ways. Apparently he didn't believe in second warnings.

I started looking through the suspect interviews. As Jason had said, the SDPD did appear to have rounded up a bunch of ex-hippies that had been involved in activist groups in the 1960's. Most of them had gone on to academia. I read through the two interviews that had been conducted with the suspected

1968 bomber first. Michael Lewis had been a chemistry professor at UCSD back in 1993. He'd denied any involvement, although he'd admitted to having met Adam Collins at an academic function. He'd described them as friendly acquaintances, if not friends. Nothing in his interviews made me think he was lying, and the SDPD had come to the same conclusion. Lewis had even been out of the country at the time of the bombing; there was no way he could have placed the bomb himself, although I supposed he always could have had an associate do it. That was going outside the bounds of things that were very likely, though.

Two other suspects were a married couple who had gone on from their activist days to become economics professors at SDSU. Again, the police had found nothing to make them suspect they'd been involved. The same held true for a fourth suspect who had gone from activism to running a hedge fund in La Jolla. Apparently he'd decided that if you can't beat the man, you join the man.

Other than the chemistry professor, nobody interviewed seemed to have been questioned for any reason other than their counterculture pasts. The cops had really been grasping at straws with this one.

I took out my laptop and looked up Michael Lewis online. There wasn't a great deal. I found a biography in a scientific journal he'd been published in that said he'd retired in 2002. There was a brief notation that he'd been part of a group called the Young American Socialists during the 60's, but the name didn't mean anything to me. They'd either kept a low profile or were very bad at publicity.

Searching for information on the group didn't turn up much, either. They'd been involved in a few protest marches against the Vietnam War, but that seemed to be about it. They'd been among a number of groups suspected of planting a pipe bomb under a police car in 1968, but the bomb had turned out to be a dud. It seemed like a chemistry professor would be better at blowing things up than that.

The Young American Socialists had ceased to exist by 1970. I'd have been embarrassed to admit I'd had to look up what year the Vietnam War actually ended, but luckily there was nobody around I had to admit it to.

It might be worth looking up the professor and meeting him, just to get a sense of him. I liked to think I was fairly good at catching people when they were lying to me. If he knew anything about what had happened, maybe I could get it out of him. That was a longshot at best, though. There was almost no reason to think he'd been involved.

I spent another hour looking through the case files, trying to come up with a plan of action. After so many years, though, there wasn't much to be done. I had no crime scene to examine. There had been no witnesses and there was no security camera footage to look through. Google probably kept track of people who searched for things like "how to make pipe bombs," but there had been no modern Internet back then. Besides, gunpowder wasn't hard to get a hold of. You could even make it yourself if you knew how.

I looked through the file until I came to the name of the lead investigator on the case: Howard Lanford. I didn't know him; that had been long before my time at the SDPD. He'd almost certainly be retired by now, if he was still living. He'd be a good starting point, though. I picked up my phone and nearly called Jason London, but then I remembered he was supposed to be off buying a crate of drugs. I dialed Miranda Callies instead, another cop from my A.A. group. "Nevada?" she asked when she picked up. She sounded shocked. "What's wrong?"

"Nothing's wrong," I said. "Why?"

"Well…you've never actually called me before."

"Oh." I thought about that. I hadn't been keeping track, but I guessed I hadn't. "So," I said. "What's new?"

"Nothing."

"Yeah," I said. "Me, too. Is that enough small talk? I'm never sure. Hey, how about those Chargers?"

"I'm a Raiders fan," she said. "Fine, enough small talk. What's going on?"

I told her I was looking into an old case and needed to contact Howard Lanford. "He's probably retired," I said. "If you can get me a current number and an address, that would be good."

"He'll be in the union directory," she said. I heard her typing.

"So…how are things in the gang unit?"

"You really don't have to make small talk, Nevada. I just figured for you to pick up the phone it had to be an emergency. I'm glad it's not, though. Okay, here it is." She gave me a phone number, which I wrote down. "His last known address is in Scripps Ranch. Looks like he retired in 2005."

I wrote down the address and tried to think of some more small talk, but I didn't have anything good. I didn't know anything about Miranda other than what she shared at meetings, and it hardly seemed appropriate to bring any of that up. "Thanks," I said.

"No problem. See you when I see you."

We hung up. I was secretly glad she hadn't brought up going to an A.A. meeting. It felt like a small victory. A small, stupid victory, but a victory nonetheless.

I was getting ready to call Howard Lanford when my phone rang. Dan Evans was on my caller ID. "What?" I answered.

"Always nice to hear your voice, Nevada," he said.

"Sorry," I said. "Hi, Dan. How are you? I'm fine. How about that sports team you like, that does all the sportsing? How are they doing?"

"Forget it," he said. "Look, I want you to hear this from me before you see it on the news. We've got another body."

"The copycat? Did the Laughing Man already catch up with him."

"No, it's another victim." He paused. "I don't want to put any pressure on you Nevada, but I think you should take a look."

"I'm busy with all the things," I said.

"Nevada…"

"These things aren't just going to do themselves, Dan."

"For god's sake, will you come take a look at this?"

"I don't know," I said. "When I see the body and don't start wailing are you going to give me a bunch of shit about how I don't react to things enough?"

He didn't say anything for a minute, but from his breathing

I could tell he was trying to keep from losing his temper. "Fine," he said finally. "I'm not going to give you shit. Maybe I was wrong to give you shit before."

"You think?"

"Don't push it, Nevada. I'm not apologizing for caring about you."

He'd gone for his trump card. "I guess all these things can wait for later," I said. "Give me an address."

He gave it to me. "Look, Nevada, this is just a heads up. This one isn't like the last one. I think you're going to react this time."

"I don't know," I said. "I'm pretty hard to impress."

Chapter 10

It took me twenty minutes to reach the address Dan had given me, which turned out to be an abandoned community park in the hills northeast of the city. Rusted play structures sat at one end of it, with a picnic area at the other. Chain-link fence posted with signs for a local construction company surrounded the entire thing. This lot was probably going to be bulldozed at some point in the near future to make way for a new strip mall, or something equally as unnecessary.

The park held so many police officers one might have thought they were having a convention. That was probably what had attracted the media, who already had their cameras trained on the scene, trying to catch a glimpse of whatever was inside. I ignored them as I made my way past the uniforms guarding the entrance. I'd rather they not get a shot of my face this time.

Dan Evans was easy to spot; with his size he'd have stood out in any crowd that wasn't made up entirely of professional football players. Sarah Winters and Brad Ellis stood at the bottom of a children's slide nearby, looking at something I couldn't see yet.

Dan moved to intercept me as I headed for the slide. "I don't want you to freak out," he said. "This one's different than the other."

"You said that already. I'm not exactly known for freaking out, Dan."

"Yeah, except for that one time you did, and you wound up in the psych ward."

I shrugged. "I don't like to do things halfway." He still looked nervous. "What?" I asked. "You don't really think this is the Laughing Man?"

"I don't know what to make of it."

"Then I'll be able to rule it out pretty quickly," I said. "There's no way this is him."

"You haven't even seen the body yet," he said.

"I don't need to. The Laughing Man isn't going to start the game when there's an impostor sitting at the board."

Dan's brow wrinkled. "Huh?"

"Oh, forget it. Show me what you've got."

Dan led me over to the slide. Sarah and Ellis stepped aside so I could see the victim lying on her back at its bottom, as if she'd just come down from the top and stopped to look up at the sky. This one was a woman in her twenties. She wore a set of flannel pajamas and had her brown hair pulled back in a bun. I couldn't see the knife wound that was almost certainly in the back of her neck, but I had a great view of her face, which had been mutilated into the Laughing Man's signature smile.

The cuts were cleaner; I was willing to bet they'd been made with a straight razor this time. The marks weren't nearly as expert as the ones the Laughing Man would have made, though. Straight razors weren't as easy to use as a precision weapon as a person might have thought. I'd spent a lot of time practicing with one when I'd worked his case all those years ago. There was a learning curve.

And beyond that, there was the obvious problem. I chuckled. The absurdity of it was just too much for me.

Sarah nearly turned white when she heard me laugh. "Good god, Nevada," she said.

Ellis watched me curiously while Dan put a hand on my shoulder. "Nevada, it's okay," he said. "Come away now."

I shook his hand off and turned to the crowd on the other side of the fence, cupping my hands around my mouth. "Hey! You dumb fuck!" I shouted. "Are you watching this? Can you hear me?" I looked around, then started yelling again. "This isn't even *close!*"

Dan grabbed me by the arm. "What the *hell* is wrong with you?" he snarled. On the other side of the police lines I could see television cameras filming our position. Odds were I was going to be on the news again.

"Oh, get off me, Dan." I shook myself free and pointed at the body. "Don't any of you see it?"

Dan looked at the body, and then back at me. "Okay. What are we supposed to see, Nevada?"

I held out my hands in front of me in a square shape, my thumbs touching like a movie director framing a shot. "Look at the piece, Dan. What do you see?"

"The *piece*?" Sarah asked. Ellis just scowled at me.

"I see a body on a slide," Dan said.

"But what does it *say* to you?"

Dan looked at me like he was trying to figure out if I'd taken up smoking crack. "It says some lunatic killed a woman."

"It doesn't say *anything*!" I said. "It's *nothing*. It's *garbage*. This is some kid playing with daddy's tools in the garage."

Dan put his hands in his pockets and glared at me. "Okay, I'll give you it wouldn't be the Laughing Man's best work…"

"What you have here is someone who wants to impress the Laughing Man so much that he's making crude caricatures of what the Laughing Man actually *does*. It's a little better this time, I'll give him that much. He's learning. But it's still garbage."

Sarah turned around and took a few steps away from me. "Okay," Ellis said. "If you're such an expert, what would *you* have done?"

"I don't know," I said. "I wouldn't go around killing people in the first place. But at least…I don't know. The Laughing Man creates still *lifes*, not still deaths. Sit her up on the slide like she's enjoying herself. Have her looking at something. Throw some props in there. Dress her up in clothes that would be a little more appropriate to what she's doing. She's in her pajamas, for fuck's sake." I snapped my fingers. "I've got it. She's in her pajamas. He should have done it at her house, instead. Sit her up at the kitchen table like she's eating breakfast. Make her coffee and muffins. Get some orange juice and cereal in there because those are parts of that balanced breakfast. If he was being really creative he could put the TV on to one of those dumbass morning shows; have it repeat on a loop so Al Roker would still be doing the weather when someone came in. That would be fucking *perfect*."

Dan took me by the arm again and started dragging me away from the scene. "I'll walk you back to your car," he said.

"What?" I asked. "You wanted my opinion."

He was practically marching me away from the body now. "You are starting to scare me," he said under his breath.

"Why?"

Dan shook his head. "Now I get why Sarah talked to me about you. You've completely lost sight of the fact that that's a person back there. It's not a painting, Nevada. It's a real life that's gone."

"I know that," I said.

"You don't appear to know that at all," he said. "I can't believe I thought you were stable enough to handle this."

"You mean you didn't bring my badge with you?" I asked. "You're not going to ask me to come back and be a detective?"

"Fuck no."

"Aw." I looked over my shoulder. Sarah and Ellis were watching me go like I was being taken to the principal's office. Well, Ellis was, anyway. Sarah had a look on her face that suggested I was on my way back to the psych ward. "Okay," I admitted. "Maybe I was a little abrupt about that whole thing."

"Abrupt?" Dan asked. "You were downright terrifying."

We reached my car and Dan opened the door for me. "I think you're overreacting," I said.

"I think we're going to have a very long conversation about this later," he said.

"Oh, good," I said. "I love long conversations. It's my favorite thing to do besides pull all my fingernails out."

"Get your ass in the car, Nevada."

I got in the car and Dan shut the door. I watched as he walked back to the crime scene. He *was* overreacting, wasn't he? I thought it over. Of course he was. Unless…maybe he wasn't. Was there something wrong with me? I hadn't laughed at a crime scene like that before. Never.

Except…I actually had. Three years ago, when I'd failed to get to the Laughing Man before he killed those two little girls. After he'd beaten me half to death. When I was on my knees after he'd walked away, looking at the blood on my hands. Watching it drip onto the floor. I'd laughed then. I'd laughed until a doctor shot me full of sedatives and knocked me out.

I took my phone out of my pocket and started to dial Molly's number. I hung up when it started ringing. This wasn't something I could talk to her about. We'd been clear that she could be my friend or my therapist, but not both. I wanted her as a friend more than I wanted her as a therapist. But I was starting to think I might be falling into a hole, and I definitely wanted to talk to someone about that.

This didn't seem like a good time to be going back to an empty motel room and looking through files. I looked at the clock and then thought about how long it would take me to get downtown. I did have somewhere else I could go. If I hurried I'd make it in time. I started the car and started in the direction of the freeway. I'd been putting this off for too long. It was time to talk to the drunks.

Chapter 11

The cops had their daily A.A. meeting in a small side room at the Lutheran church downtown. I think the Lutherans probably used it for Sunday school. I'd never asked. I hadn't been to a religious service since I'd been a child, and I was in no hurry to start back up again now.

I reached the church just before 5:30. Jason London was on his way in and spotted me coming up the steps. "I'll be damned," he said. "I didn't think we were going to see you in here again anytime soon."

"I just really missed you guys," I said. "You know how sentimental I get."

"Yeah, that sounds like you."

"How did it go with the drug bust?"

"About like you'd expect," he said. "They sold me drugs. My guys came in and arrested them. They seemed really surprised."

"Some people never learn."

"Good thing, too. I'd be out of a job." He started to smile but it froze when he took a good look at my face. "You all right?"

"Yeah. Rough day, I guess."

"I guess that explains why you're here," he said. "Well, you're in the right place."

Inside the room was the usual rogue's gallery of ex-drunks with guns I'd come to know and...kind of like, anyway. Love wasn't my thing. Mike Brown, a former detective from Robbery who'd been busted down to patrolman for drinking on the job sat next to Miranda Callies. Half a dozen other cops in and out of uniform sat on folding chairs that had been arranged in a wide circle. Most had Styrofoam cups of nasty black coffee in hand. I stopped at the table near the door to pour myself half a cup of the black stuff. I only drank regular coffee at A.A. meetings, never really having cared for it. I didn't think the group was going to bring in an espresso machine just to accommodate me.

I took a chair in the circle and sat down while Mike Brown read from one of the laminated sheets that had the A.A. steps and traditions printed on them. It was always the same routine at the beginning of meetings, and probably had been since...I didn't actually know. I hadn't read a lot of the organization's history. A.A. had gotten its start in the 1930's but at first it had been a couple guys just sitting around talking. The printed stuff had come later. I didn't know if it could be amended like the Constitution, or if it had been set in stone for decades.

After the recitation of the steps and traditions, Paul Wilkins, who had been the training officer of at least three people in the room, opened up by asking if anyone had anything they wanted to get off their chest. He looked pointedly at me as he did so. I didn't say anything. One of the patrol officers spoke up instead and spent a few minutes talking about her marriage. When she was done we went in a circle, taking turns to speak. Nobody had anything earth-shattering or life-changing they needed to talk about. For some people, meetings probably had much the same function of going to a therapist or a priest would. You could talk about whatever you wanted to and nobody in the room was going to break your confidence. It also had the advantage of being free, and there was no priest to assign you a penance if he didn't like what you had to say.

When the circle got to me I said, "My name's Nevada. I'm an alcoholic."

"Hi, Nevada," everyone said in unison.

"I'm not sure why I'm even here today," I said. "I guess it's that I've been to two crime scenes this week and looked at two bodies, and now everybody thinks I'm crazy."

Miranda nearly gasped. "You got your badge back?" Everyone turned to stare at her. Interrupting someone while they were speaking was strictly taboo. "Sorry," she said.

"Forget it," I said. "I'm not back with the department. I guess I'm a consultant, or something like that. The thing is..." I took a second to think. "I'm not reacting to it. Or I'm reacting *wrong*, I guess. I was out looking at a woman with her face sliced half off and I started trying to taunt whoever was responsible for it. Shouldn't I be...I don't know. Sad? I mean, not falling apart, obviously. I'd have made a pretty shitty cop if I got weepy every time I saw a dead body. But I'm not a cop now. I see these dead people and I just don't give a shit about them. It's not any different than looking at cat litter." I thought about that for a moment. "I think I might be broken," I said. "Anyway, that's all I've got to say today. Thanks."

The meeting continued until everyone had had a turn to speak, and then Paul brought things to a close with the Serenity Prayer and a reminder that anything said in this room was supposed to stay in this room. My coffee had gotten cold; I'd forgotten to drink it. As people shook each other's hands and started drifting out, Miranda Callies came over and sat down next to me. "It's good to see you here," she said.

"I just really missed sitting in a circle," I said.

"No, you didn't." She smiled. "Did you call Howard Lanford?"

"No," I said. "I got busy with this damn copycat thing. I'll try him tomorrow. It's not time-sensitive. I mean, unless he dies of old age before I reach him. I'd feel pretty stupid about it then."

Paul stepped over to us. "It's good to see you, Nevada," he said. "How long has it been?"

"Two weeks," I told him. "But you'd think I died, the way you people react."

He took a seat next to Miranda. "When someone disappears from this circle it's not hard to imagine they've gone back out again."

"Fair enough," I said. The group had had its share of relapses. Every now and then somebody would stop coming in for a while, and then they'd be back to start their A.A. medallion collection all over again. I was coming up on four months sober. There was no way in hell that was going to happen to me.

"You said two crime scenes?" Paul asked. "Is this the copycat, or does Homicide bring you in on everything these days?"

"It's the copycat," I said. "I started laughing when I saw the body. Dan's mad at me. And Sarah Winters is probably afraid of me by now."

"Sarah understands that you and she approach things from very different places," Paul said. "Very few people have had your...well, why don't we say your experiences give you a *unique* perspective?"

I stared at him. "Sarah talks to you about this?"

"She does," he nodded. "She thinks the world of you, and she likes to consider you a friend." He smiled. "Don't worry, Nevada. I don't repeat anything you, or anybody else, says in this room. Sarah's been like a daughter to me, though. When she needs to talk, I listen to her."

"She's such a Girl Scout," I said.

"Are you saying she's not your friend?"

"No," I said. "I'm not saying that. I don't know why she's working homicides, though. She's good at it, but she'd probably have been a better kindergarten teacher."

"I can't say that never occurred to me," Paul nodded.

Mike Brown came over and shook my hand as he headed out, as did another of the patrol cops. "Did you ever meet Brad Ellis?" I asked Paul.

"Once or twice," he said. "I've heard he's a good

detective."

"He's a preening douchebag," Miranda said.

"I've also heard that," Paul admitted. "I'm sure I didn't hear it in here, though."

"It doesn't matter," I said. "Sarah can hold her own. Anyway, I didn't really come in here to talk about the case. It's just...I don't know why I'm like this."

"Depression?" Jason asked from where he'd been saying goodbye to another cop. "They make pills for that."

"Maybe you shouldn't be the person to talk to me about pills," I said.

He shrugged. "I didn't mean the stuff I was on. You know doctors actually prescribe medicine for people. Half the department is on something or other."

"Nevada," Paul said. "Why did you start drinking?"

"I don't know."

"Yes, you do."

I scowled at him. "Fine. I drank so I could sleep at night. And later I drank because it was the only way I could get through the day. Because I hated the person I was and the booze made me forget about that person. It's not rocket science."

"No, it's not. I think you know what we call it."

"We call it self-medication," I said. "I've read the book, Paul."

"It's not in those same words," he said, "but the fact is, the reasons you drank didn't just go away when you put the bottle down. We don't just magically become different people overnight. We just become people who don't drink anymore."

"I don't know if that's better or worse," I said. "At least when I was drinking it didn't bother me."

"You also didn't have the chance to make any changes," Miranda said. "I didn't know you then, but I heard you were pretty much living in a cave waiting to die."

"It wasn't a cave," I protested. "I hadn't vacuumed in a while, sure, but there wasn't *that* much mold on my carpet."

"It was a metaphor, Nevada. Sort of."

"I know." My phone buzzed and I looked at the caller ID. Dan Evans was checking in. I could ignore him for a while, but he'd never stop calling until I talked to him. "I should go," I said. "I've got a couple things I need to do." I looked around at the three of them. "Thanks for being here."

"That's what we do, Nevada," Paul said. "And you're here for us, too."

"Well, good luck to *you* guys, then." Anyone who called me when they were having a crisis was going to have it rough. I wasn't good at that kind of thing. Unless they were calling because they needed me to shoot someone. That much I could handle.

Chapter 12

I called Dan back as I was walking out to my car. "Shut the fuck up," I said when he answered. "I don't want to hear any more of your shit. I went to a meeting and you're not my fucking therapist."

He was silent for a moment. "Okay," he finally said. "I was actually going to apologize for being short with you earlier. You didn't deserve that."

"Oh," I said.

"Anything else you want to get off your chest, Nevada? I've got time if you want to yell at me some more. It's not like I have a fucking job to do or anything."

"No."

"Well, take your time and think about it. Maybe you want to tell me I'm a fucking asshole because I care about you?"

"No."

"No? Wait, I've got it. How about that I'm totally out of

line for being worried when you act like a crazy person and start shouting at nobody at a crime scene. In sight of fucking *television cameras*, for god's sake?"

"I said I was sorry."

"No, you didn't, Nevada. You didn't say that. You never say that."

I sighed. None of the fights I picked with Dan ever went the way I planned for them to. "I'm sorry, Dan. I shouldn't have snapped at you like that just now. I'm frustrated with myself and I took it out on you."

He was quiet for a long moment. "Wow," he said. "That was good. Did you rehearse that apology?"

"No."

"Did you see it on television? Read it in a book?"

"Give me a break, Dan."

He chuckled. "I was kidding, Nevada. Mostly. You aren't exactly known for your apologies."

"I like to think that's because I'm right so often."

"It's not. Anyway, forget it. You have any thoughts on the copycat? CSI is going over the scene with a fine-toothed comb but I don't think we're going to get much."

I unlocked my Mustang and got inside. "You were right before."

"How?"

"This one was different enough from the first to be interesting. The body wasn't dumped and the facial wounds were done better, even though they obviously weren't the

Laughing Man's work."

"You don't think we've got two of these lunatics out there?"

"Two copycats? No. Just one. I think the killer is learning."

"Learning how?" Dan asked.

I needed to come up with a way to explain this that wasn't going to make me sound like a psychopath. "He's learning that the Laughing Man's signature isn't the way he mutilates the face. That's part of it, of course, but the real signature is the art. Sarah knew that even before she called me out there for the first body. She already knew it was a copycat. She just wanted me to confirm it. The killer didn't understand that. Now he's starting to get it."

Dan thought that over. "Weird," he said.

"Yeah. I'm not sure why he didn't get that in the first place, but I guess it's not the first thing that catches your eye. You see the faces he carves and not the scene he's set up. Forest for the trees, I guess. But even if he'd posed the body better it wouldn't have fooled me. It's a hard thing to do right."

"The art?"

"Yeah. I don't really know how to explain it. It's like a forgery. Even if it's done really well, an expert is always going to spot it."

"And you're the expert," Dan said.

"Unfortunately. But the copycat, whoever he is, is so amateur at this you're not going to need me. If you get any more bodies before Sarah catches him I'll come look at the crime scenes. I'll help any way I can, but I don't think I'm going to have much to give you. Sarah can call me if she needs any advice. I don't care if it's the middle of the night. It's not like I ever sleep that well."

"I'll tell her. Thank you, Nevada."

"I'm all about being helpful," I said.

"And I'm glad you went to a meeting."

"You know something?" I asked. "I think I am, too."

I drove out to a strip mall I knew in Mission Valley to pick up take-out Chinese food, a carton of pot stickers and another of their house chow mein. Back at my motel I sat down in front of my laptop to eat and screw around on the Internet. There were funny cat videos to watch, and as much as I'd never have admitted it to anyone, I liked funny cat videos. I also spent a good half hour watching some PBS show where a guy visited bed and breakfast hotels in New England and talked about why he liked each one. I had no idea why I found *that* appealing. Maybe it was the idea of getting away from San Diego, but I certainly wasn't going to New England anytime soon. If I was going to get on a plane and disappear, it would be to somewhere tropical. And isolated. Somewhere nobody could find me.

I thought about getting a cat. Maybe once my house was done and I moved in it would be worth considering. I was sober now and could probably handle the responsibility of taking care of an animal. If I'd had a pet during my drunken years it wouldn't have had much of a chance. I'd barely been able to remember to feed *myself* back then, let alone anyone or anything else.

Molly sent me a text saying she was sorry she'd missed my

call and asking whether I needed anything. I was a shitty friend in that I only got in touch with people when I was a mess. I texted back that everything was good and I'd catch her another time.

Sooner or later I was going to have to drag myself back to a therapist's office. Why did I keep putting it off? Stubbornness? That sounded about right. I had things to do first, though. Tomorrow I'd get in touch with the cop who'd worked Anita's case back in the 90's. Maybe he'd have some ideas. If he could just give me a placed to start, maybe I'd have somewhere to take the investigation. I'd never expected it to go far, but I'd expected it to go farther than *this*. The files Jason had given me had been next to useless.

I wasn't that surprised to see I'd made the ten o'clock news. They ran a clip of me with my hands cupped around my mouth, shouting at nobody like a crazy person. The microphones hadn't been close enough to pick up anything I'd said, thank god, but it didn't look good. I was surprised that no reporters had called me to try and get a comment. Then again, it wasn't easy to get my number. No cop who had it would have been willing to give it up for fear of my reaction, and one of the advantages of living in a motel was that it made you hard to find. If someone did track me down, I could always leave and check into another motel under a fake name. Celebrities were able to get away with that, weren't they? To keep the paparazzi away? I wasn't a celebrity, but I had a gun. Two guns, actually.

Just before I went to bed I shut off all the lights in my room and then went to peek out the window. There was no activity in the parking lot. Nobody was sitting in a car alone for no apparent reason. No suspicious vans were around. Maybe the Laughing Man wasn't watching me. Maybe his attention was focused on the copycat and he'd forgotten all about me.

It was a nice thought, but I knew it wasn't true.

Chapter 13

I picked up a breakfast sandwich from a gas station the next morning and headed back to the motel to call Howard Lanford. His phone rang four times before a woman answered. "Lanford residence."

"My name is Nevada James," I said. "I used to be with the San Diego Police Department. I was hoping to speak with Mr. Lanford about an old case of his."

"I'm sorry, Detective, but Mr. Lanford is resting at the moment. You'll have to call back..."

I'd been about to interrupt and tell her I wasn't a detective anymore, but an old man's raspy voice barked, "Who is that?" before I had the chance.

There was a noise on the phone as if the woman was putting her palm over the phone's handset, not that that kept her voice from coming through. "It's not important, Mr. Lanford. You're supposed to be resting now."

"I won't be told who I can talk to in my own damn house,"

Lanford said. "Give me the damn phone."

A moment later I heard his voice clearly. "Who is this?"

"Is that how you talk to your wife?" I asked him. "You're lucky she doesn't cut your throat."

"She's not my wife," he said. "She's my nurse. Now who is this?"

"Nevada James," I said. "I'm…"

"You're that crazy woman from the television," Howard interrupted me. "I saw you yelling in the park like some damn hobo."

I sighed. "Okay, that wasn't my best moment ever. Anyway, if you have a few minutes…"

He cackled. "I was playing with you, Detective. I know exactly who you are. Can't say I know why you're calling me, though. I never worked a serial killer case. Or are you people so desperate now you're calling old men out of retirement?"

Of course he'd known who I was. Even if I hadn't once been the most famous cop in San Diego, I'd been on television twice in the last week. The last time hadn't been particularly flattering. "No, but I'm not calling about that. I should also tell you I'm not a cop anymore, either."

"I know. You went down like a shooting star."

During my drinking days I'd have taken mortal offense to that comment, but he wasn't lying. "Fair enough," I said. "I'm calling about the Collins case from 1993. The car bomb."

Lanford exhaled slowly as if I'd just poked him with a pin to let the air out of him. "Let me guess," he said. "Anita hired you."

"Good guess."

"Not really. You couldn't be working it in an official capacity. How did you get your hands on the case file?"

"I said some magic words and they appeared," I told him. "It was really weird. Anyway, I've got a few questions, if you don't mind."

"Why don't you come up here?" he asked. "I'd like to meet you."

I shrugged, then remembered he couldn't actually see me. "I can do that. SDPD gave me your address. When is good?"

"Now is fine. Julia is trying to make me take a nap, but you'll be on important police business, so it's just too bad for her."

"I'm not a cop."

"She doesn't need to know that. See you soon, Detective."

Scripps Ranch was just north of me on I-15, not far from Miramar. It took me twenty minutes to get up there and find Lanford's house, a modest split-level ranch in the suburbs. I parked on the street and went to ring the doorbell. A tired-looking woman in her fifties with gray hair pulled back in a bun answered the door. She wore a pink lab jacket with the name of some medical outfit on it. "You must be Detective James," she said.

"That's me."

"I'm Julia. I'm his nurse. Do you have a badge you need to show me or something like that? I don't know how these things work."

"I'm not here to arrest anyone," I said. "We just need some

help with an old case of Mr. Lanford's."

She nodded. "You may as well come in, then, and good luck to you. He's feisty today."

Julia led me into the kitchen. Howard Lanford was waiting for me there, a cup of coffee on a circular wooden table in front of him. He looked to be in his seventies and probably weighed 120 pounds, which I was guessing was down from at least 180 or more, given his frame. He sat in a wheelchair with a blanket over his legs and had a clear tube under his nose feeding him oxygen. It was looped over his ears and attached to a tank on a rolling carrier that could be pushed along with him.

Lanford pointed to an empty chair at the table. I sat. "That's enough, Julia. You can leave us alone now. We have important police business to discuss." Julia nodded, somehow refrained from rolling her eyes, and left the room.

Lanford looked me up and down. His breathing was on the ragged side. I'd made a joke about needing to talk to him before he died of old age. I felt pretty shitty about that now. Lanford didn't have a lot of time left.

He finally grunted. "You don't look like much."

I shrugged. "Neither do you."

Lanford glared at me for a moment, then his face cracked and he exploded into laughter that degenerated into a coughing fit a second later. When he recovered he said, "No, but I'm dying. What's your excuse?"

"I was drunk for three years."

He held my gaze for a moment and then nodded. "I guess you really were. I'd heard that, but you know how people talk.

I thought maybe some of it was a fish story."

"No," I said. "That was a true story. If anything it was worse than whatever you heard. I damn near died."

"I won't offer you some Scotch, then."

"You drink Scotch for breakfast?" I asked. "I do that, my old boss picks me up and carries me to the hospital."

"I'll be dead in a few weeks," he said. He nodded at his coffee. "So I put a little in there when nobody's looking. Julia pretends she doesn't know. She does, of course, but she also knows it hardly matters anymore."

"Fair enough."

Lanford reached for the coffee. His hands shook a bit, but from the way his lips pressed together in concentration I could tell he was putting on a show of force, trying not to let me see how bad it really was. He probably hadn't been exaggerating about how much time he had left.

He took a sip of the spiked coffee and sighed deeply, then slowly put the cup back down. "Tell me what you think of Anita," he said.

I shrugged, not ready to show him my cards.

"She's a sweet old lady, isn't she?" Lanford asked. "Did she make you cookies and tea? I always liked her cookies. Rum raisin was my favorite."

"There was tea," I said. Lanford nodded at me encouragingly. "I guess I didn't rate cookies. Maybe I should have stuck around longer. I was kind of hoping she'd read me a story and tuck me into bed."

Lanford threw his head back and laughed. "Good," he said.

"You're not a complete idiot."

Julia poked her head into the kitchen. "Everything okay in here?"

"We're fine," Lanford snapped. "Let us be, woman!" Julia retreated.

"You could be nicer to her," I said.

"I'm leaving her everything in my will." He gave me a stern look. "And don't you dare tell her that, either. I want it to be a surprise."

"I'm sure it will be," I nodded. "So we've established that neither of us bought Anita's kindly old grandmother act."

"Oh, she wasn't always like that," Lanford said. "When I met her the first time, in the hospital, she was exactly who I expected her to be. Scared, mourning, in more physical pain than I'd ever wish on a person. It took years before…" he looked away. "I don't really blame her, mind you. She waited for justice for a long time. But every time I saw her, she was just a little bit angrier with me."

"Frustrated, I'm sure."

"Yes. The investigation stalled out after the first few weeks. I kept trying, of course, but we burned up all our leads." He winced. "Maybe I shouldn't have said *burned*. Anyway, I kept going back to her with nothing. And then one day, the anger was gone. It looked that way, anyway. She smiled. She touched my hand. She told me she knew I'd been working hard for her and she appreciated it."

"When was that?"

"Maybe ten years in. I kept digging the file out every now

and then, and then I'd go by and tell her we still had nothing. And she was so…warm. So kind."

"She…" I thought about how to phrase my next question but didn't come up with a delicate way to ask. "Did you two…you know…"

"No!" he said. "Good god, woman!"

"I was wondering if she tried to seduce you," I said. "I wasn't saying you'd try to take advantage of her."

"Well, neither of those things happened. We talked and drank tea and she was cheerful. She asked about my family and laughed when I told her about my new grandchildren. It wasn't until later…she slipped once, and I got a look at her eyes." He frowned. "She was lying."

"Lying?"

"She wasn't warm, or understanding, or enjoying any of my silly little stories. She wanted blood. Mine, I thought."

I blinked in surprise. "You think she wanted to *kill* you?"

"Maybe. For failing her. I let the killer go free." He shook his head. "And she was right, of course. After that I just called her now and then to let her know what was going on. I didn't want to see those eyes again."

"You obviously don't think she was involved, then."

"No." He shook his head again. "No chance. Not with that kind of hate. And you'd better understand this, Detective." He wagged his finger at me. "She's been carrying that torch for twenty years. She'll never give up. She'll never stop."

"I was getting that idea," I said. "Tell me about the suspects you had."

"None of them did it."

That hadn't been what I'd expected to hear. That maybe he suspected someone and couldn't make a case, sure. Not that he'd just dismiss them outright. "You're sure? You cleared all of them?"

"They were a bunch of useless old hippies. The only one I ever seriously considered might have done it was Lewis, the chemistry professor. We knew his group built a couple shitty bombs during the war, even though they never managed to get one to go off."

"One of them was found under a police car, if I remember."

"You've done your homework. Another dud. Even if it hadn't been, the FBI never had anything to tie it to him directly. They spent enough time looking. And he kept preaching that 'fight the power' nonsense after he became a professor. Served as a faculty advisor for a socialist group on campus. We had him on tape saying violent action was sometimes the only catalyst for social change."

"But you cleared him?"

"He was in Europe at the time of the bombing. He'd been there for three weeks. He knew Adam Collins socially but claimed not to know much about his work, and he didn't seem to give a good goddamn about some supercomputer nuking everyone, or whatever the bomber was afraid of. We had no reason to think he was lying. And to be honest with you, he was the type that if he'd done it, he'd want you to know. It would have been a statement."

"Maybe I should talk to him anyway."

"If you see him, tell him I'll see him soon."

"Oh?"

"In Hell," he said.

I sighed. That would teach me not to take my research more seriously. I'd never gotten as far as an obituary. "I only knew he'd retired. When did he die?"

"Couple years ago. I only knew because I read the obituaries every day. It's a morbid habit I picked up when I got sick. I keep waiting for my name to show up."

I thought things over for a minute. "Well, shit," I said. "That means I've got nothing."

"Welcome to the club," Lanford said. "Don't worry. We don't collect dues."

"Maybe we should have jackets made. We could wear them around town and hang out with the guys who were looking for Jimmy Hoffa."

"Hoffa's in a gravel pit in Camden, New Jersey."

"What? Really?"

"No." He smirked. "Got you, Detective."

I drummed my fingers on the table, trying to think if there was anything else worthwhile I could ask. Lanford took another sip of his coffee and frowned. "Can't really even taste this anymore," he said. "Even with the Scotch. I just drink it out of habit." He gave me a long look. "Do you carry a gun, Detective?"

"You know who I am, so you know the answer to that question. Why?"

He smiled weakly. "I don't suppose you'd put it down on the table and leave the room for a few minutes?"

I felt my heart break just a little bit. "You know I can't."

Lanford shook his head. "Ah, well. I doubt I'm strong enough anymore to pull the trigger, anyway." He sighed deeply. Never get old, Detective."

"There's really no chance of that," I said. "If the Laughing Man doesn't kill me, the shit I've done to myself drinking will."

"You should take up smoking, just to be sure."

We looked at each other for a moment, and then we both started to laugh. "I like you," I said. "I don't say that to a lot of people."

"Now you're just trying to get into my will," he said. "Sorry. Julia gets everything. She's put up with me for a lot longer than you have."

"I guess I'll just have to retire on all this Mafia money I have stashed away."

Lanford frowned at me. "Mafia money?"

"Forget it," I said. "Long story. Anyway, have you come up with anything since you retired? Any leads you were never able to track down?"

He bit his lip as he thought it over. "Not really," he said. "Although...I was never sure about the bomb."

"The bomb? Because of the hydrogen peroxide that turned up in the analysis?"

"No, that was a lab mistake. There was never any hydrogen peroxide. The weird thing was that the bomb should never have been able to do as much damage as it did."

"I don't know a lot about pipe bombs, but it was hard for me to imagine one taking out a car."

"Oh, they can. Pipe bombs are what terrorists use to blow up convoys in Iraq. But those are big ones filled with shit you make in a lab. This one was small, and it was maybe half full of gunpowder. It was going to go *bang*, of course. But take out a car and burn that way? That hot? No. That never sat right with me. There were times I thought that thing was never supposed to explode the way it did."

"Who sets a bomb and *doesn't* want to blow something up?" I asked.

"I never figured it out," Lanford said. "You like riddles, Detective?"

"No."

"Well, here's one anyway. When is a bomb not a bomb?"

I thought it over. If it wasn't supposed to blow up, what else was a bomb good for? "When it's a message?"

"Good," Lanford nodded. "Or when it's a warning, I would think."

"And what's the message?"

He shrugged weakly. "I have a bomb?"

Or maybe the message had been about the smart computers the note Anita had found warned of. The note the bomber had left obviously hadn't stopped Collins from continuing his work, so maybe the bomb had been meant as a second, more serious warning. My mind wandered back to the Unabomber case. Kaczynski had railed against what he called the "industrial-technological" system when he wrote his manifesto. If I remembered correctly, he'd called for a revolution against technology. The Collins bombing fit that profile almost perfectly. But the FBI had ruled Kaczynski out as a suspect. They wouldn't be wrong about that.

"Another damn copycat?" I mused.

"What's that?" Lanford asked.

"Never mind," I said. "I've got to do some reading."

"And I think it's finally time for me to take that nap," he nodded. "Forgive me, Detective, but I'm very tired. I'm sure you understand."

"I do," I said. I stood up. "Thank you for your time, Detective Lanford."

"You're very welcome, Detective James." He smiled at me and extended his hand, which I shook gently. His skin was dry and fragile, and it felt as if I could break the bones in his hand if I squeezed too hard. On impulse, I suddenly leaned over and gave him a quick peck on the top of his head. "Naughty girl!" he said. "You're still not getting my money."

"See you again?" I asked.

He shook his head. "I don't think so, Nevada. But if you get anywhere on this before it's too late let me know, will you? I'd like to know how it works out."

"I will."

"Good. Now tell Julia to get her ass in here on your way out, will you? She needs to earn her inheritance."

"Take care of yourself, Howard. I'll be in touch."

Chapter 14

I was already three miles away when I realized I should have pushed harder about the lab report. If it wasn't hydrogen peroxide they'd found in the bomb, then what was it? That residue hadn't come from nowhere.

And how was it the FBI had ruled out the Unabomber? This kind of thing seemed right up his alley. They knew something I didn't, obviously.

I took my phone from my jacket pocket and dialed the police switchboard. "This is Nevada James. Can you connect me to the FBI office on Vista Sorrento?" I was fairly sure they still had their San Diego office there. It had been a while since I'd been in touch with anyone from the Bureau.

There was a moment of silence, probably while the operator tried to decide whether to remind me I wasn't a cop anymore and shouldn't be calling this number, but then there was a click and I heard ringing. "FBI," a woman's voice answered almost immediately.

"Special Agent Carter, please," I said.

"Special Agent *in Charge* Carter is out of the office," the operator said. "Can I ask who's calling?"

"Nevada James."

The woman on the other end of the phone hesitated. "Was that you on television the other night?"

I sighed. "Could you ask Special Agent *in Charge* Carter to call me when he's free? He's got my number." I hung up on her. In hindsight I wasn't sure whether Carter still had my number or not, but if the FBI couldn't figure out who it was that just called them, what use were they?

I'd just gotten back to my motel when the phone rang. I didn't know the number on the caller ID, which meant answering it broke my unwritten rule about answering the phone if I didn't know who was calling, but there were only so many people it was likely to be. "Hello?"

"I'll be damned," Llewellyn Carter said. "How the hell are you still alive, Nevada?"

"It's a goddamn mystery," I said. "Have you really missed seeing me on television the last few days? I've been told it's pretty amusing."

"I don't see a lot of local news," he said. "Are you calling about the copycat thing? It's not really on our radar."

"No." I gave him a quick rundown on the Anita Collins case. "I know you guys looked at it and ruled out the Unabomber. I'm trying to figure out why. From my perspective, he'd have been a fantastic suspect. You must have had something good."

"I've never heard of the case before," he said. "I can get the file, though. But tell me why I'd do this for you?"

"Because you owe me," I said.

"I owe *you*? You broke my goddamn nose, Nevada."

I wasn't surprised he was still mad about that. "You deserved worse than what you got," I said. He made a grunting noise. "Do you really want to have this fight again?" I asked. "Because you'll lose. Tell me what's in the file and we'll call it even." I thought about that. "Actually, no, we won't. You're still going to owe me. You'll just owe me a little less."

He was quiet for so long that for a minute I thought he'd hung up. "Hello?" I asked.

"Are you ever going to forgive me, Nevada?" he asked quietly.

"No."

He sighed. "I'll pull the file and get back to you. Or did you want to meet somewhere?"

"No. Just call me. I don't need to see photos." Actually, I just didn't want to see *him*. I might be tempted to break his nose again.

"Fine." He hung up.

I sat on the motel bed and drank a Diet Coke. Maybe I'd been too hard on Llewellyn. He wasn't a bad guy. I'd liked him very much once. I'd even trusted him, and trust wasn't something I'd ever just given away. That was what had made his betrayal so painful. Llewellyn had thrown a roadblock in my path at the worst possible moment while I'd been on the Laughing Man case. He'd have said he'd done it because I'd been out of control and needed to be reined in, but people were dead because of it. I'd never be able to let it go.

It took Llewellyn two hours to call me back, just when I was getting into a Discovery Channel show about a bunch of people who lived in the middle of the forest and still somehow managed to get into all manner of shenanigans. I had no idea what it was called. It seemed like that sort of thing made up a lot of the Discovery Channel's programming.

I picked up the phone. "What do you have?"

"We don't even exchange pleasantries now?" he asked.

"You know what's weird?" I asked. "A minute ago I was thinking about why I don't like you, and it made me like you even less. Is that normal? Now stop wasting my time and tell me what you have."

He sighed. "The bomb design was wrong for the Unabomber. Shorter pipe, wrong width, lower yield, although actually better put together, like the bomber had a better idea what he was doing but didn't really want to hurt anyone."

"Better designed? Kaczynski did manage to blow up a lot of people."

"His designs weren't up to this level. He built his bombs out of scrap metal and garbage, basically. From what they recovered of the bomb that killed Adam Collins and his son, we could tell whoever built it had access to better equipment. I wouldn't call it a pro job, but it's like comparing a blunderbuss to an early modern rifle." I snickered. "What?" he asked.

"You said *blunderbuss*."

"It's a good analogy. Also, there's nothing to indicate he'd ever heard of Adam Collins. Collins wasn't even well-known in

San Diego back then. The academic community locally *might* have heard of him, but that would be it. Beyond that, we put together a timeline for Kaczynski after we caught him. He was nowhere near San Diego at the time of the bombing. It wasn't him. Open and shut."

I thought about it. "Okay, fine. Lower yield but better designed? What's going on there? I've seen photos of their car. It was practically melted."

"Yeah," he said. "That's weird. I don't think the bomb was supposed to do much besides go *bang* really loud and throw up some smoke, but it blew the hell out of that car. It shouldn't have been able to. Which sort of points at this other thing."

"What?"

"There was a substance found that nobody could identify."

"The stuff they thought was hydrogen peroxide?"

"But it's not. You can't put hydrogen peroxide in a bomb, and this isn't it, anyway. I've got part of a chemical analysis but I don't know what the hell it means. The lab at the time said it's not something that exists on Earth."

"Of course," I said. "That explains everything. It was aliens. Aliens came down here and blew up Adam Collins."

"Yeah. You're a genius, Nevada. Well done."

He sounded bitter, and I decided I didn't care for his tone. "You want to try a fall with me, Llewellyn?" I asked.

"No."

"Because it sounds like you're getting a little uppity with me. You're not getting uppity with me, are you?"

"No, Nevada." Now he just sounded glum.

"Good. I want a copy of the chemical analysis."

"You want to meet me now?"

"No. Fax it to me at…" I got the motel's fax number off the panel on the phone and gave it to him. "I'll see if I can make any sense of it."

"Fine. It'll be there in a few minutes."

"Good. Anything else you can tell me?"

He hesitated. "Just that…I'm sorry, Nevada. I thought I was doing the right thing."

He wasn't talking about the Collins case anymore. I didn't want to talk about the thing he was talking about. Part of me wanted to tell him it was okay. I'd have been lying, but it would have been a nice gesture on my part. Maybe it would help him sleep at night. But I just couldn't. "Honestly, Llewellyn, I don't know if I could have gotten to those two little girls before the Laughing Man killed them. I really don't. But I do know the time you cost me getting to them meant I never had a chance. I'm never going to get past that."

"I know."

"So don't try to make it sound like I'm the asshole here."

"I'm not, Nevada, but I don't think I'm the asshole here, either. I just wish things had worked out differently."

"Yeah. So do I. Fax me that stuff. I'll talk to you…I don't know. I was going to say *later* but it's not like I'm putting it on my calendar."

"Goodbye, Nevada." He hung up.

I sat there with my phone in my hand for a few minutes. I wanted to call him back. I also wanted to put my phone through the window. I decided to put it in my pocket instead. That seemed like a smarter move.

I waited ten minutes and then walked over to the motel's front office. The clerk there handed me the papers that had come without a word. He liked me. I paid my bills in cash and didn't make any noise or throw my trash into the parking lot. I was his ideal tenant.

Back in my room I took a look at the papers Carter had sent over. The bomb residue had been analyzed; none of it was anything out of the ordinary except a substance that was classified as "unknown." Part of a chemical structure had been diagrammed next to it. I knew enough chemistry to recognize the difference between hydrogen and oxygen atoms, but that was about it. Nor did the formula the FBI had come up with, full of O's and H's with numbers in superscript, mean anything to me. How that would have been used in bomb making was a mystery.

I didn't know any chemists I could go ask about this. But it occurred to me I did know someone who knew a great deal about bombs. I'd arrested him a long time ago. Maybe it was time I paid him a visit.

Chapter 15

San Diego County had just one state prison within its borders, which sometimes surprised me given the county's sheer size; it was the second largest in California. As a result, most of the prisoners from the area wound up being shipped to other parts of the state. The one I wanted to see had been up in Pelican Bay for a year or two, but they'd moved him down here closer to his release date.

I drove out to Donovan Correctional Facility early the next morning. The prison was in Otay Mesa, just a few miles from the Mexican border. There were around 3,000 prisoners locked up there, most of them with names nobody would recognize. Although the last I'd known, Robert Kennedy's assassin, Sirhan Sirhan, was in custody there. Knowing that wasn't going to get me a spot on *Jeopardy!*, though.

It wasn't visiting day, but I pulled strings. My visitor's badge identified me as an SDPD contractor, which I figured was close enough to the truth that I didn't mind the lie. Did the SDPD employ contractors? Maybe to fix the plumbing in the men's room, but I couldn't imagine for much else. I'd been off the force for long enough I really couldn't have said for sure.

I sat alone in a small waiting room that looked like a condemned school cafeteria while the guards retrieved the prisoner I'd come to see. As much as I knew I was in no real danger here, leaving my Glock behind at the security desk had nearly given me a panic attack. I felt naked without it. Even sitting here alone, I could almost feel the Laughing Man's fingers on the back of my neck. Somehow I doubted that feeling was ever really going to go away, even if I managed to put a bullet in his head before he got me first. I'd probably take that fear to the grave.

A security door opened and a prisoner in a red jumpsuit stepped through, followed closely by a guard half his size. The guard was built like a football player, but the guy I'd come to see was practically a giant. He'd have dwarfed Dan Evans if they'd been standing side-by-side. He'd started shaving his head since the last time I'd seen him, and his ebony skin glistened with sweat. It wasn't hot in here. He'd probably been in the gym, unless he'd taken to oiling his head, which seemed unlikely.

He spotted me immediately, which was easy enough given that there was nobody else in the room. His brow wrinkled in confusion and he looked for a moment like he wanted to turn and leave, but the guard behind him prodded him forward, which looked a little to me like a sheep poking a lion. I motioned to the seat across from me at the circular table I'd been sitting at. After a moment, he crossed the room and sat down.

"Big Leonard," I said. "It's been a while."

Leonard gave me a sullen look. "You know I don't like to be called that. Every time you were on the stand it was 'Big Leonard this' and 'Big Leonard that.' Drove me nuts."

"Yeah, I know," I said. "It's just...you're so..." I looked at him and spread my hands apart like I was measuring his shoulders. "Big."

He glanced at the two papers I'd placed on the table before he'd gotten here, then back at me. "What do you want, Detective?"

"I'm not a detective anymore," I said. "This is a private thing."

"You're kidding. You went P.I.?"

"No. I'm just...shit, I don't know. I'm looking at an old case for someone I know. There's a formula on that paper; it's something that was used to make a bomb back in the 90's. Nobody knows what the hell it is." I pushed the papers toward him.

His eyes flickered toward the papers and I knew he was struggling to keep his curiosity in check. "Why would I help you with a case?"

"Because you don't hold a grudge that I put you in here?" I sighed. "Don't tell me you're holding a grudge, Leonard. It's beneath you."

Leonard pursed his lips. "No. I don't hold a grudge. You were doing your job. I was doing mine. But that doesn't mean we're old friends and I'm going to do you a favor out of the kindness of my heart. Are you offering me time off my sentence?"

"Nope," I said. "I have no legal authority here."

"Then…what?" He looked at me expectantly.

"I'll show you my tits."

He blinked like I'd set off a flash bulb in his face. "What? Really?"

"Of course not," I said. "These walls must be messing with your head if you thought there was a chance of that happening. What I *will* do is fill your commissary. You can buy yourself all the smokes you want."

"They don't let us smoke in here," he said.

I shrugged. "Well, that's probably for the best. I've heard it's bad for you. Also, putting you near an ignition source would have to be the stupidest thing they could do in here."

Leonard smirked. "You really think I can't get my hands on an ignition source, Detective? I could blow this place off the map with the shit they keep in the kitchen, if I wanted to. I don't want to. I have 17 months until I'm up for parole, and then I'm out of here."

"17 months?" I frowned. "Seems like it should be longer than that."

"I got a lot of good time."

I nodded. "You were always polite," I said. "And I guess in here nobody wants to start anything with you. You look like you could break through the wall like the Kool-Aid Man."

Leonard rolled his eyes as I waited for him to say something, then gave in. "Oh, yeah," he said with mock enthusiasm, just as we'd both known I'd hoped he would. People who were willing to do impressions of the Kool-Aid Man for me couldn't be all bad.

"Anyway, then that's 17 months I'll fill your commissary. If you play nice, maybe I'll even testify for you at your first parole hearing."

He raised his eyebrows. "That would make a difference," he said. "Would you really do that?"

"I don't know," I said. "Would you promise to turn over a new leaf when you get out of here? Get a job, pay your taxes, and, I don't know, maybe never blow anybody up again?"

He shook his head. "No."

"Then I won't help you get out. But I'm good for the money. You have my word on that."

Leonard watched my eyes for a moment, maybe trying to run some kind of psychic lie-detector test on me, then he turned to study the papers in front of him. His brow furrowed as he thought. For two full minutes he didn't move, and then he chuckled.

"What do you see, Leonard?"

He looked back up at me. "This was in the 90's?"

"Yeah."

"That's why nobody knew what it was. It didn't exist back then. It doesn't exist *now*, at least not in this form."

"They thought it was hydrogen peroxide for a while."

"No. That's just dumb." He shrugged. "I guess I can't blame them, but...dumb." He pointed at the formula. "You see this? I wouldn't have guessed what it is except for the peroxide bridge, which is..." he stopped and looked at me. "No offense, but maybe you want me to give you the easy version?"

"I think that would be best, Leonard."

"Okay." He thought about it for a minute. "You know oxygen bonds are highly unstable when they're chained together, right?"

"No."

"Well, they are. They're almost...I'll put it like this. You ever heard of high-test peroxide?"

"It's possible I'm going to need the *really* easy version of this, Leonard," I said.

He sighed. "Okay. High-test peroxide used to be used as rocket fuel, but basically it's just concentrated hydrogen peroxide. Most people wouldn't get near the stuff. You could try to synthesize some in any modern lab, but you so much as look at it wrong and it's going to blow you away."

I nodded. "I get it. So someone got their hands on rocket fuel and used it to make a bomb."

Leonard looked at me like I'd suggested unicorns had been behind the bombing. "No. Of course not. I was just using the example so you'd understand that oxygen bonds are unstable. This isn't high-test peroxide, but it's *a* peroxide."

"I don't mean to be rude here," I said, "but I think I'd also like the *short* version of this story."

Leonard crossed his arms in front of him and smirked at me. "Fine. You want to know what this is, Detective?" He leaned forward conspiratorially. "It's malaria medicine."

I crossed my arms to mimic him and smirked back. "I can also have them *take away* your commissary, Leonard."

"I'm serious."

"Explain it to me like I'm an idiot, then, because I clearly am."

"Artemisinin is a drug. It's used as a treatment for malaria." He tapped the paper. "This is a variant form of it. I might not have recognized it, but the peroxide bridge gives it away. That's where this oxygen bond," he pointed and then frowned at me, "forget it. I can tell by its structure. If it's not unique, it's damn close. I'd bet you anything whoever came up with this was working with artemisinin in a lab. They were probably trying to come up with a new delivery system. How that would have worked I don't know. That part's beyond my expertise."

"Artemisinin. So...it's medicine that makes people explode. I guess that would take care of the malaria part of the problem." I glared at him. "This is some Bugs Bunny shit, Leonard."

"Well, it's not exactly artemisinin, anyway, but even the real stuff I wouldn't light on fire if I had it in its pure form. But nobody takes it in its pure form. Once it's in a larger molecule with water or whatever they use, it's more stable. So you can put it in a syringe or a pill. The real stuff actually comes from a plant they found in China a while back. You ever seen a plant explode?"

I thought about it. "No."

"Same thing. But you refine and refine and refine, you might come up with something you weren't expecting. Whoever made this probably wasn't looking to make a bomb. They just noticed they had something that went bang if you hit it right. But if you made a mistake with your formula, or you used too much, it's a whole different thing."

"Okay," I nodded. "So I'm looking for a scientist." Michael

Lewis, the only suspect Howard Lanford had ever taken seriously, had been a chemistry professor. He was dead now, but I still had a lead. If I could tie him to the bombing, I'd be able to put this thing to bed.

Leonard smiled. "I did good, right? You sure you don't want to show me your tits, Detective? I think I might have earned it."

"I'll send you a *Playboy*," I said.

"They don't let us have porn in here, either."

"Really?" I asked. "What do you guys do in here all day?"

"You want me to tell you?" he shrugged.

"No," I said. "I don't think I do. Anything else you can think to tell me?"

"If you find the guy who did this, tell him to look me up. I want to talk to him when I get out."

"I don't think I'm going to do that." I stood up and collected my papers. "Thank you, Leonard. Really. I'll load up your commissary on the way out."

"I appreciate it."

"If you think of anything else, make a call to the police switchboard and have them transfer you to me. They'll know how to get in touch." I gave him a serious look. "That'd be worth something to me, Leonard. You understand?"

"You could just give me your number, Detective."

"I could also start working as a phone sex operator, but that's not really likely, either." I nodded at him. "Take care of yourself, Leonard. Try not to blow anything up in here."

"I'm not going to blow anything up anytime soon." He smirked. "Not for 17 months, anyway."

Chapter 16

I thought about what Leonard had said on the way back to my motel. Michael Lewis, although deceased, was my most likely suspect in the bombing. If I could establish that he had anything to do with artemisinin research, this would be over. He had the radical background, after all. That couldn't be a coincidence. But to prove it I was going to need access to his work. Odds were that would only be available at a research library at UCSD.

That presented a problem. I was neither a teacher nor a student at the university. I needed access to material that wasn't going to be accessible to the general public. I could hardly walk in there and start poking around. But odds were what I'd need would be accessible in their computer system. I didn't know anything about computer hacking, but I knew several people who did.

My phone buzzed as I was driving. It was a text from Sarah Winters. *Can you talk? Have a weird idea on the copycat case. Could use your ear.* I put the phone down. I'd deal with that later. I didn't really want anything more to do with that case. Given my reaction at the last crime scene, who knew what insanity I'd get up to at the next one.

Back at the motel I got out my laptop and used a program I had to access a proxy server that would both encrypt everything I did and conceal where I was doing it from. As far as any average person would be concerned, I was now connecting from an Internet café in Belgium as opposed to a motel room in San Diego. It wouldn't fool the NSA, but I didn't need to fool the NSA. They didn't have any reason to be looking for me. Even if they had, they certainly weren't going to care about any of this.

Once my connection was up I logged into a webmail account I kept for this purpose. It identified me as someone named Trevor Sebastian, which was a name I'd made up a few months ago. I liked to imagine Trevor was the dashing playboy type, maybe sipping a glass of champagne while he looked over his stock portfolio from his own private island somewhere. Not that it mattered much, but it had seemed like Trevor needed a backstory, even if I never told it to anyone.

I opened a new email message, putting "Abercrombie" in the "to" field. *Need help*, I typed as the subject. Then I saved the email as a draft. It was never going to be sent to anyone.

That over with, I turned on the motel television and watched half an hour of *The Price is Right*. Nobody won a new car. The show seemed pointless to me if nobody won a new car.

When the show was over I went back to my laptop and looked at the message I'd typed earlier. The word "what" had appeared in the message body. I wasn't the only person with access to this account, which was the whole point.

I thought it over, then started a new line in the message. *UCSD faculty research, professor Michael Lewis, anything on antimalarial drugs or development, artemisinin, variants of artemisinin, explosive properties, peroxide bridge (?), possible explosive applications.* That was about all I could think of, but it seemed like it covered everything. I saved the draft message and waited.

A moment later more text appeared. *Is this one of your stupid jokes?*

No, I typed, and saved the message again.

A minute passed. *If this is a joke, tell me now. You get full credit for the funny, but I'm not wasting a day on this only to have you throw a pie in my face.*

I'd never actually thrown a pie at the man I was typing to, but given some of our history he wasn't wrong to be suspicious. *No joke*, I typed. *Research for Anita Collins bombing case in 1993. Bomb composition suggests chemist doing malaria research. I know it sounds stupid. Deal with it.*

I waited. It did sound like a joke, of course. I'd hardly believed it, myself. But my jokes tended to be a bit more elaborate and less science-based.

Will contact appeared on the screen. *Confirm.*

Confirm, I typed. A second later the entire draft email disappeared, erased and lost to cyberspace.

Fake emails that never got sent weren't the most secure way to communicate under the radar, but it would do. We weren't planning to blow up an airplane. If Abercrombie had really been concerned, it would have been a very different conversation.

I had very little else to do until I was contacted again. On a lark, I picked up my phone and dialed Anita Collins. She answered on the second ring. "Hello, Nevada."

"Have you ever heard of Michael Lewis?" I asked. "He was a UCSD professor."

"I can't say that I have," she said. "Is he a suspect?"

"Maybe," I said. "He's been dead for a while, but so far he's the best lead I have. I should know more in a little while. I was just wondering if the name was familiar. If maybe he was someone you or your husband knew."

"I don't remember the name, but we do have any number of donors affiliated with UCSD."

"It could be nothing. Believe it or not I've got a guy checking to see if he was involved in malaria research. I know that sounds stupid, but there could be a connection. Don't ask me to explain it, though. Chemistry wasn't my subject."

Anita was silent long enough I started to wonder if we'd lost the connection. "Hello?"

"I'm sorry," she said. "It's just that one of my foundations supports malaria programs in South America and Africa. It's a massive project. That seems like quite a coincidence."

I thought it over. "It's *a* coincidence," I said. "I don't know whether it's significant. I would think a lot of charities fund malaria programs, and you yourself probably fund more programs than anyone could remember."

"I suppose that's true," she said. "I may look through my records and see if I can find this Mr. Lewis, though. We started funding the drug distribution…maybe ten years ago. One of my donors came to me with the idea."

"Was he by any chance a chemist?"

"No. He owns a soccer team."

"Probably not a mad bomber, then," I said. "I'll let you know if I come up with anything. It's too late to put him behind bars, but at least you'd know the truth."

"That's all I want, Nevada. I can be satisfied knowing the truth."

"I'll let you know as soon as I know something."

"Thank you for the call."

"No problem." We hung up. I looked over at the dresser drawer where my vodka was stashed. It wasn't even afternoon yet, way too early for my nightly booze-holding ritual. It was tempting, regardless, but I decided it could wait until later. The day I needed to pour two glasses of vodka down the drain to make it through the day would probably be the day I drank one of them.

My phone buzzed. It was Dan Evans texting this time. *Channel 5 asked where you are. They want an interview.*

When hell freezes over, I sent back.

That's more or less what I told them. Clever boy, that Dan.

There was a knock at my door. I took my Glock off the bed. "Who is it?"

"Tapestry Flowers," a man's voice called back. "Delivery for Nevada James."

Only one person ever sent me flowers. It had been a little while since he'd done so, which probably made me overdue for an arrangement. I fingered the Glock and went to look through the window. A teenage boy in a blue polo shirt stood just outside my door with a bouquet in his arms. The coast seemed to be clear of anyone else.

I opened the door, holding the Glock behind my back so the kid didn't see it and wet his pants. "For me?" I asked. "How sweet."

The teenager smiled halfheartedly. The flowers were carnations in a variety of cheerful colors. "There you go, miss," he said, offering them to me. I liked that he called me *miss* instead of *ma'am*, but I was never going to admit that to anyone.

I took the flowers in one arm, keeping my gun hand behind my back. "I don't suppose you have any idea who sent them?" I asked, scanning the parking lot behind him to see if anyone was watching.

He shook his head. "I just deliver them. There's a card on there, though. Have a nice day."

I shut the door and watched through the window as he walked back to his car. There was no other activity in the parking lot. The Laughing Man could be sitting somewhere farther away with a set of binoculars if he'd really wanted to see my reaction, but somehow I doubted that was the case. The Laughing Man didn't do things like this to get a reaction out of me. He did them because, in his own twisted way, he genuinely cared.

I put the bouquet down on the table and sat the Glock next to it. Carnations seemed a little pedestrian for the Laughing Man, but maybe he had decided to change things up. Or maybe I had a secret admirer. That didn't seem all that likely, though. Had Llewellyn Carter worked out where I was and decided to send them as a peace offering? No. He'd have had to know I'd just set them on fire and send him the ashes.

The card was in a small white envelope. Someone had written *Hope You Like These!* on it. Underneath the words they'd drawn two little hearts.

My stomach did a flip-flop. I sat the card down on the dresser, then picked up the Glock and went back to the window to look outside again. Nothing had changed.

I thought for a minute about what to do, then I went to the dresser, took my vodka out, and tossed it into my suitcase. My laptop followed it, along with my toothbrush and everything else I had in the bathroom. I jammed my dirty clothes in on top and zipped the suitcase shut. The .45 Dan had given me went on my hip and the Glock found its place in my shoulder holster. I looked around. That was everything I had in here other than my Laughing Man files, and I wasn't going to try to move them now.

There was no small amount of nostalgia involved in leaving the room. It had been home for a while. There was no way in hell I was staying here, though, and it was hard to say when I'd be back, or *if* I'd be back. I took a last look at the flowers on the table and then headed for my car.

I called Dan as I drove up I-15. "What's going on?" he answered. "Don't tell me you actually want the interview?"

"I'm disappearing," I said. "Go to my motel and get my files. You shouldn't have any trouble getting a key from the desk. The guy likes me. Don't tell him I'm checking out, though. As far as anyone else is concerned I'm still there."

Dan inhaled sharply. "What the hell is going on?"

"Someone sent me flowers today."

"The Laughing Man? That's nothing new. Why are you running? Did he make a threat?"

"That's the thing, Dan," I said. "They weren't from the Laughing Man. They were from the copycat."

"What?"

"He knows where I am, Dan. He knows me. I don't know what this is yet, but...I guess I'm part of it now." I couldn't think of anything else to say. "I'll call you in a while."

Dan started to say something but I hung up and tossed the phone onto the seat beside me. I didn't feel like talking. I felt like shooting someone. Talking was just going to have to wait.

Chapter 17

I ignored half a dozen calls from Dan as I drove up the freeway. He finally gave up, which I took as a good sign. He'd be on his way to the motel to see what was what. Meanwhile, I needed to find a new place to live. I obviously hadn't been careful enough last time. That was what I got for checking into a hotel under my own name. It was time to be someone else. Julia Roberts, maybe.

How the hell did Julia Roberts check into hotels anonymously, anyway? Most places made you show identification. Somehow I doubted she had a fake driver's license. Or maybe she did. The truth was I didn't know much about Julia Roberts.

I made a stop at my bank and took out ten grand in cash. I wouldn't be using plastic to pay for anything for a while. Debit and credit cards were easy to trace. Cash was anonymous. Anonymity had just become even more important to me than it had been before.

The only reason I was still alive today was that the

Laughing Man valued playing our game more than he did just killing me outright. He'd had me at his mercy twice and could have ended me with a flick of his straight razor. But doing that meant the game was over, and he didn't get to have any more fun. He'd never find a playmate he enjoyed as much as he did me. The copycat was another situation entirely. What that unstable asshole was up to I didn't know yet, but I didn't have a way to hunt him and the cops hadn't gotten very far. Sarah was still asking *me* for advice, which meant she had nothing. Death didn't scare me; I'd accepted that I was going to die young a long time ago. Dying for nothing bothered me a great deal, though. Having some idiot walking up behind me and sticking a knife in my neck wasn't the way I wanted to go out. I'd either die by my own hand, or by the Laughing Man's. Nobody else got to dance with me.

I found a motel near Miramar that looked like it was on the edge of being condemned. Compared to this place my old motel was the Ritz Carlton, but this one had good sight lines of the parking lot and the nearby streets. It would do. I went into the office where an older man in his 60's sat behind a desk that also looked to be falling apart. For a moment I thought I saw a group of cockroaches doing aerobics in the corner by the copy machine.

"I need a room," I said. "I'll pay cash up front."

The old man looked me up and down. "It's thirty-five dollars a night. Includes tax."

Those were flophouse rates for San Diego. "You rent by the week?" I didn't plan to stay long, but I didn't want to ever be in this filthy office again, either.

"$240 if you want a week."

I counted out five hundred-dollar bills onto the desk. "Give me two weeks. Keep the change."

The clerk glanced at the cash but didn't make a move to take it. "You a drug dealer? You don't look like a drug dealer."

"I'm someone who wants to be left alone."

"Prostitute, then? I don't care, mind you. You wouldn't be the only one here. I just don't want trouble in the parking lot."

I stared at him. "Do I look like a prostitute?"

"They never do, at first." He shrugged. "I'll need an ID."

I put another hundred on the desk. When he didn't say anything I added another, and then another on top of that. "Fine," he said. "Forget the ID. You were never here."

"I don't want housekeeping knocking on the door."

He snorted. "That's not going to be a problem."

I gave him a serious look. "If anyone asks about me, or comes by here looking for a woman my age and describes me, it would be worth something to me to know about that. You understand? If you got me a description of whoever it was, or footage from a security camera, that would be worth even more."

The clerk squinted at me. "You famous or something?"

"I'm Julia Roberts."

He laughed. "You're pretty, but you sure as hell aren't Julia Roberts. I'll keep an eye out for you. You need anything, let me know." He looked out the window at my Mustang. "You come in that?"

"Yeah. Don't take down the license plate number. Just

make sure I don't get towed."

"They don't come unless I call them. You got a dead body in the trunk or something?"

"Not yet. It's still early, though."

My phone buzzed as I was lugging my suitcase into the first-floor room I'd been given. It was Dan calling again. "Hey," I answered.

"I'm in your room," he said. "Where are you?"

"Gone," I said. "Gone like the wind. Wind that was in a hurry, even."

"Damn it, Nevada…"

"I'm near La Jolla," I lied. "Don't worry, I'm not going to hide from you. Just everyone else. You see the flowers?"

"Yeah. The card is a dead giveaway. How did the copycat find you?"

The Laughing Man had been sending me gifts for years, usually with a card attached. On the card he'd write a friendly message, and he always drew a laughing face. The drawing wasn't any more elaborate than a circle for a head, with a few lines sketched inside to make eyes, a nose, and a mouth, but it was always the same. He'd never drawn a heart. Even if he'd been sane enough to entertain romantic feelings for me, he'd have considered that an inelegant way to express them. "I was staying under my own name there," I said. "I figured the Laughing Man would be able to find me if he really wanted to, but I didn't think anyone else gave a shit."

"Someone else does," Dan said. "I'll get this over to the forensics guys. We probably won't get a fingerprint, but maybe they'll find something we can use."

"I doubt it," I said.

"So do I."

"He did do the card himself, though, so he'd have had to go into the flower shop. Maybe someone would remember him."

"I'll check it out. Tell me where you are."

"No."

"*What?* You just said you weren't hiding from me."

"I'm not," I said. "I'm hiding from the fleet of patrol cars you'll send to babysit me the minute you know where I am."

He paused just long enough to try to think of a good lie. "I wasn't going to do that."

"Wow," I said. "That was the best you could do? You are the worst liar of all time."

"Nevada…"

"You could have said, 'Nevada, I respect your judgment and would never try to force bodyguards on you,' or something like that."

"Nevada…"

"Wait, I know," I said. "You could have tried, 'Nevada, we live in dangerous times, but as long as you *promise* to be careful I'll respect your wishes.' See, that might have worked. You'd have been playing on the fact that you know how seriously I take promises, so if you managed to get one out of me, you might think I'd believe you in turn."

Dan didn't say anything for a long minute. I imagined if I

cracked an egg on his head right now it would fry in a great hurry. "You okay, Dan?" I asked. I liked needling him a bit, but this was a time it was important not to go too far. If I did, he might be willing to go as far as defying department protocol and having my cell phone traced. And if he did that, shortly afterward he'd be wondering why their tech guys *couldn't* get a location on my phone. I wasn't about to tell him about the modifications that had been made to it. He'd start wondering what kind of company I was keeping.

"All right, Nevada," he finally said. "But I am going to want to see you. I'll call to check in after I hit up the flower shop."

"Sounds good," I said.

"And what are you going to do until then?"

"I don't know," I said. "I'll think of something."

Chapter 18

My new motel room looked like the kind of place junkies go to die. It stank of carpet cleaner that had been applied far too liberally, maybe to cover the smell of something else that was better left not thought about. I didn't bother unpacking my clothes; I didn't want them exposed to any of the surfaces in here, anyway. After a cursory check of the bathroom, I decided I'd be taking my showers at Molly Malone's dojo. For that matter, maybe I'd go to a hardware store, buy a roll of plastic sheeting, and cover every surface in the room with it. I was pretty far from being a clean freak; my house had reached the point of moldy carpet back in my drinking days, when I'd been too drunk to pick up my garbage, but this was ridiculous.

I put the .45 and my Glock down on the bed. As much as I really didn't care for the .45, it wasn't going to kill me to have a backup piece. I didn't really expect that any of this was going to come down to a gunfight, but you never really knew what was going to happen. If my life had a theme, it was that whatever could go wrong absolutely would, sooner or later. Sometimes it seemed like the world was out to kick me in the teeth.

I'd made a mental note of all the cars in the motel's parking lot when I'd come in. Now I looked out the window and checked for any new ones. Nothing had changed. If the copycat had been waiting at my other place and followed me here, he'd had the sense to stalk me from somewhere I couldn't see him.

Why he would send me flowers was an interesting question. The Laughing Man had done that for years, starting shortly after I'd gotten his case. That was hardly common knowledge, though. I didn't think it had ever made the news, but that was something I could check on. Fewer people knew he'd kept doing it after I'd been kicked off the force and holed up in my house to drink myself to death. Dan Evans, Sarah Winters, and...I thought it over. That was about it. Some of the lab techs had known, certainly. Back when I'd still cared I'd passed things the Laughing Man had sent to me on to them in the hopes that they might find DNA, or a fingerprint, but none of those things had ever panned out and eventually I'd just given up on it. Llewellyn Carter knew. He'd taken it personally back then. There was little doubt others at the FBI were aware of it. And people did talk, after all, even when they knew perfectly well they were sharing things they weren't supposed to. Want to show off your importance to your friends? Impress them with your insider knowledge about the most famous serial killer in San Diego history. The court jester always knows some of the king's secrets.

I looked through the window again. One car that had been here when I'd arrived was gone now. Nothing else looked different.

I was getting hungry and didn't feel like having food

delivered. I didn't know Miramar nearly as well as I did some of the other neighborhoods in San Diego, so I wasn't sure where to pick up groceries around here, either. I hadn't brought any food with me, though, so I decided to head out to explore. It didn't take me long to find a Ralph's. I went inside and picked up a 12-pack of Diet Coke, a tray of pumpkin muffins topped with chocolate chips, and half a rotisserie chicken. If I'd been a grown woman that would have made for a pretty pathetic dinner. Oh, wait. I *was* a grown woman. Well, too bad. I'd have a kitchen once they finished building my house, but damned if I was moving in there before they caught the Laughing Man's copycat. Two people had died in my last house inside of a week. The new one was going to stay a corpse-free zone for as long as I could manage it. As long as *my* corpse didn't wind up in there, I'd have nothing to complain about.

When I left the store I saw a red convertible had parked next to my Mustang while I'd been inside. I wasn't that surprised to see a model-beautiful young man leaning up against its door waiting for me. Another equally beautiful young man sat behind its wheel, not looking in my direction. That was Fitch. He never looked at me.

"Hey, Abercrombie," I said as soon as I was within earshot. He tossed his head to the side, sending his silky blond hair tumbling to the side like an ocean wave. If he hadn't been gay I might have jumped on him right there.

"You do know my name isn't Abercrombie?" he asked.

"And his isn't Fitch," I said, nodding at the other young man. "But you won't tell me your real name, so you get to be Abercrombie. Hey, Fitch," I called to the driver. Fitch continued not looking at me. "I don't think Fitch likes me," I said to Abercrombie.

"He likes you. He just has trouble expressing himself. We're working on that."

I couldn't tell if he was making a joke or not. Abercrombie tended to be very…dry. "Well, I guess that's a good thing."

Abercrombie and Fitch worked for Scott Landers, a somewhat retired computer hacker who had made a fortune stealing from the bank accounts of the rich and unpleasant. Now he managed money instead of stealing it. Scott's brother had been an early victim of the Laughing Man, which was how I'd come to know him. Technically, given that I'd discovered what Scott's past had entailed, I should have introduced him to my friends at the FBI, who would no doubt have loved to meet him and offer him free lodging at the supermax prison in Florence, Colorado, for the rest of his life. But I had a certain sympathy for the Laughing Man's victims, and the truth was I didn't really care what Scott had done. He didn't kill people, and his skills had proven to be extremely useful in my work. He was the reason nobody other than his people could get a location on my cell phone, and that was the least of what he could do.

My phone buzzed with another text from Sarah Winters, asking to meet me as soon as possible. I put it in my pocket. She was going to have to wait.

"Is that your dinner?" Abercrombie asked, nodding at my grocery bag. "Because that is just *tragic*, my dear. Do you want me to take you out and teach you how to order food in a restaurant? It's not complicated. Even you should be able to get the hang of it."

"Hey, Fitch?" I called. "When you dump this guy, I'll have

a line of hot boys just waiting to meet you. Say the word and it's done." Fitch continued ignoring me, but I thought I saw him smirk just a little bit.

"Be nice," Abercrombie said. "Do you want what I have or not?"

"Of course I want it."

"As far as I can tell, Michael Lewis kept his nose clean after his hippie days. He was the faculty advisor for some anarchist club called the Malatesta Group, and he was on record saying violence has a legitimate place in effecting social change, but all the club did was march around with their garish little signs and shout about divestment whenever the university's regents had a meeting. I expect it was one of those college things where everybody goes on about 'the revolution' for four years and then forgets all about it once they start getting a real paycheck. Kind of like the 'gay until graduation' crowd."

"Gay until graduation?" I asked. "That's a thing?"

"It's a thing," Abercrombie said. "I could tell you some stories about..."

"No, you can't," Fitch said. I think it may have been the first time I'd ever heard him speak.

"Yeah, I actually don't care," I said. "What about his work? Anything on oxides or malaria medicine?"

"His research was mainly on cadmium selenide particles. Before you ask me what that is, I don't know. I do know it doesn't explode."

I sighed. "Damn it. So this was a complete waste of time?"

Abercrombie cocked his head and grinned at me. "I could

have just called and told you that. I wanted to see your face for the next part." He waited while I stared at him expectantly. "Oh, you're no fun at all, Nevada. You could at least pretend to be excited."

"I'm excited on the inside, I promise."

Abercrombie rolled his eyes. "One of Lewis's students had several papers published that dealt with peroxide bonds. *Special* peroxide bonds. Can you guess what he was working on?"

"Artemisinin?"

"Artemisinin was his starting point, but he came up with a synthetic that makes artemisinin look like leeches and bleeding. He's changing the world."

"Yeah," I said. I had a gnawing feeling in the pit of my stomach, like a hungry animal had taken up residence there.

"More than that, he doesn't even charge for it. He's been giving the treatment away. It's all done through this foundation I've forgotten the name of..."

"I think I can probably guess it," I said.

"The man's singlehandedly responsible for saving thousands of lives. He's pretty much Gandhi, Nevada."

"Oh, learn some history," I said, a bit more sharply than I needed to. "Gandhi didn't actually cure anything. He'd have to be more like Salk. Or Norman Borlaug, maybe."

"I know Gandhi didn't cure diseases, Nevada."

"Yeah, I just wanted to sound smarter than you for a change."

"Oh, yeah? How's that working out for you?"

I shrugged. "Not so great. I think my day is about to go to shit. What's this guy's name?"

"Conrad Meyers. He retired early and sits on the boards of directors of half a dozen companies that do medical research. Lives up in Del Mar." He reached into his pocket and pulled out a slip of folded-up paper. "I even got you an address."

I took the paper and looked at it. "Thanks," I said. "I guess I owe you one."

"You owe me several, but who's counting?" He made an "o" shape with his mouth. "Wait, I know! Scott's counting! He wants to know what's going on with the copycat case."

"If he knows it's a copycat, why does he care?" I asked.

"I guess he wants to hear you say it's a copycat and that screwing around with this amateur isn't distracting you from your more important work, which is gutting the Laughing Man like a fish."

I crossed my arms in front of me. "Do I look distracted, Abercrombie?"

"Unless you think Conrad Meyers is the Laughing Man, you kind of do."

I looked over at Fitch, but if I'd thought I was going to get some backup from over there, that had been a mistake. "He's not. I'll be on the Laughing Man as soon as he actually *does* something, but right now I've got nothing to go on. He's been quiet since he sliced Chandler Emerson up at my house."

"Doesn't that seem strange to you?" he asked.

"A little. I wonder what he's waiting for. But I also don't know if he's even still alive. He could have been hit by a car last week and we all read his obituary without even knowing it. When the Laughing Man moves, I'll move. Until then, we're in intermission."

Abercrombie watched my face for a second, then looked away. "I already know the answer," he said, "but I was told to ask. Are you sober?"

I stared at him. "I said I know the answer, Nevada," he said, shrinking away as if he thought I might hit him.

"What do you think?" I asked.

"Yes," he said. "I remember you when you were a drunk. You looked like you'd been in a concentration camp. And my *god* but you stank, Nevada."

I nodded. "Fair enough. Tell Scott thanks for the concern, and the help. I'll be in touch when I have something new for him.

Abercrombie nodded and looked back at Fitch. "We're going to get going. Good luck with Conrad Meyers. I doubt he's going to have many good days left."

"Why is that?"

"Because when I told you he was changing the world, you made a face like...like you were having the best dream of your life and you just realized you were about to wake up."

That did seem about right. "Maybe," I said. I held up the paper he'd given me. "If this is the guy I'm looking for...well, I guess I really hope he's *not* the guy I'm looking for. Because if he is, I'm going to ruin his life."

Chapter 19

Del Mar was only about twenty minutes away from the motel I was hiding out in, but it was getting late and I still had half a rotisserie chicken in my bag that I wanted to eat before it got cold. Conrad Meyers could wait. I doubted he was going anywhere.

I hadn't bothered to get paper plates or plastic forks at the store, so I wound up eating the chicken with my fingers while I watched the evening news on the motel's tiny television. There was nothing new on the copycat killer. Nor were they running any footage of me screaming in the park. Hopefully the media were on their way to forgetting about me.

My phone buzzed. It was a text from Dan that read, *No joy with Tapestry Flowers. Buyer wore a hat and kept his head down. White male.*

Serial killers were almost always male, and white guys in San Diego were about as common as sunny days. I went to wash my hands before I texted Dan back. *Maybe you should investigate hat dealers.*

Smartass, he sent back. *You okay?*

Fine. May move again tomorrow. Let me know if you get anything new.

Will do.

I was about to go back to picking at the chicken carcass when the phone rang. It was Brad Ellis this time. It occurred to me that I'd been ignoring Sarah's messages. Maybe she thought I was mad at her. "Hey," I answered.

"Sorry to bother you, Nevada," Ellis said. "We've got another crime scene. Can you spare us some time?"

I sighed. "Look, Brad, I don't mean to be a bitch, but I don't see what I can contribute to this. Sarah said she had some ideas. She's a good detective. You seem okay enough. What do you want me to do here?"

"We just need another pair of eyes," he said. "I wouldn't ask you if it wasn't important."

"Fine," I said. "Tell me where."

Ellis gave me an address in Balboa Park and hung up. I looked at the phone for a moment, thinking things over. I really didn't feel like looking at another body. Nor did I really want to see Dan right now, and it was almost certain he'd show up at the crime scene sooner or later. He might try to bundle me up and put me on a plane to South America, no doubt while lecturing me on the need to keep safe.

Still, it might be better to make an appearance. I just needed to remember to keep my cool, not let my emotions get away from me, and most of all not to completely flip out and start yelling at people that weren't there. A good display of sanity and reasonableness might be enough to keep Dan off my back for a while.

I tucked my Glock into its shoulder holster and put the .45 Dan had given me on my hip. He'd be happy to see I was carrying it. I almost looked like a real cop.

Once outside I rolled the Mustang's window down so I could feel the night air. It tended to relax me, and being relaxed would be a plus once I got to the crime scene. Traffic was light and I managed to find the address Ellis had given me within about fifteen minutes. It was a small, one-story house in a residential neighborhood that had seen better days, but not so bad people would be afraid to walk down the street after dark. I recognized Sarah's car parked in the house's driveway. It was the only one there. A few other cars were parked along the streets in either direction, but this was a residential neighborhood. Cars were *supposed* to be parked here. None of them were police cars, though. I didn't know what Ellis drove, but nothing here appeared to be an unmarked police car, either.

I got out of the Mustang and looked up and down the street. Everything about this place looked like just another pleasant night in San Diego. There were no cops anywhere in sight. I couldn't hear any sirens in the distance. There was no yellow tape set up around the house. Either I was in the wrong place, or this wasn't a crime scene at all.

The address on the house was the one Ellis had given me, though. I was in the right place, unless he'd gotten the address wrong. I took my cell phone out of my pocket and unlocked it so I could dial Dan's number. He'd know about a new murder by now. If I was in the wrong place, that was one thing. But if this where Ellis had sent me...

A man's voice came from behind me. "Drop the phone, Nevada."

I lowered the phone to my side without turning around. "I'm not dropping it," I said. "It was expensive. Besides, with the modifications I had made, it'd be damn hard to replace."

"I said drop it."

"And I said go fuck yourself." I tossed the phone through the Mustang's open window. "There. Good if I turn around now, Brad?" I turned around before he had a chance to answer. Brad Ellis stood there. He had a gun in his right hand pointed at me in a traditional gunfighter's stance. It wasn't all that accurate a position to fire from, but he didn't really need accuracy at this range. With the gun at his side, it would be hard for anyone at a distance to see what he was doing. We'd look like two people chatting.

I looked at the gun. It looked like a Walther to me. Whatever it was, it wasn't his service weapon. That would have been too easy to trace.

Ellis smiled at me. "Surprised?"

"I don't surprise all that easy," I said. "Sing something from *Evita* and I'll be surprised."

He looked almost disappointed. "I'm standing here with a gun pointed at you."

"Sure," I said. "But as traps go, this isn't all that great."

"Fair enough. I had something else planned, but my timetable got pushed up kind of abruptly. Sarah's a much better detective than I thought. Now give me the .45."

It had been a reasonable gamble that Ellis wouldn't be

willing to drop me out here in the street over not breaking my phone, but leaving me with a gun was another matter entirely. I reached for my hip slowly, then took the gun from its holster with my thumb and forefinger. "On the ground," he said. I knelt down, holding my arm at an angle so my jacket wouldn't swing open. When it was on the pavement and I'd stood back up he nodded. "Kick it over here." I kicked the gun to him. He picked it up and stuck it in the front of his pants like he thought he was in an action movie. If he wasn't careful he'd blow his dick off. Not that I'd have minded if he did.

"Is Sarah still alive?" I asked.

Ellis nodded. "Of course. This wouldn't have been any fun if it was just the two of us. The game has to have a prize, doesn't it?"

"Wow," I said. "You're just...bugfuck, aren't you?"

He ignored that. "In the house. Walk ahead of me, nice and slow. Don't do anything we'll regret."

"It's pretty much guaranteed one of us is going to regret this shit," I said. But I let him march me up the walkway to the house. The door was unlocked and he was careful to stay out of my reach as I opened it, just in case I turned and tried to attack him with my hands. The man had done his homework; I had to give him that much. The last guy I'd hit had suffocated to death on his own broken trachea.

The front door led into the living room with a kitchen area off to the right. I didn't bother taking off my shoes. I looked around as Ellis shut the door behind us and turned the deadbolt. The furnishings in here were modest but functional. The one couch in the room was worn through to the padding in a few places, and the television was at least a decade old.

Everything in sight was dusty and there was a staleness that suggested nobody had cleaned in here in a long time. It reminded me of my old house, back when I'd been drinking and not bothering to take care of anything.

"Dining room," Ellis said.

I walked slowly, scanning the room for anything I could use against Ellis when the time came. The smell of fresh garlic suddenly distracted me. Either Ellis was afraid of vampires or someone had been cooking in here very recently. There was no sign of whoever lived here, though. Or whoever *had* lived here. I suspected the house's owners might not be around anymore. Whether they'd left of their own accord or Ellis had killed them remained to be seen. Possibly in the dining room. He'd brought me here for a reason, after all.

The dining room table was rectangular and had been covered with a tablecloth featuring a muted flower design. Three places had been set, and three dinner plates with a meal of steak, a potato, and vegetables had been placed on the table. Three wine glasses had been filled, and a decanter with the remainder of a bottle of red sat nearby. He'd even set out a basket for dinner rolls.

In other circumstances, even if Ellis *had* been the Laughing Man, I might have been tempted to sit down and eat something. The food smelled a lot better than my supermarket chicken had. But the sight of Sarah Winters duct-taped to the chair at the head of the table, another piece of tape covering her mouth, was enough to put me off the food. She was alive, eyes wide, and looked as terrified as I could remember ever seeing another person. Not that I blamed her.

The whole setup looked oddly familiar, but it took me a

second longer than it should have to place it. In my defense, I'd been pretty well plastered the last time this had happened. "You really are a copycat," I said to Ellis. "You recreated my dinner with the Laughing Man."

"Have a seat," Ellis said, motioning to the empty chair on the far side of the table with his gun. I walked around Sarah and sat down. Sarah kept her eyes on me as I went by, then looked back at Ellis. He sat down across from me. "What do you think?" he asked.

I looked around. "It's better," I admitted. "You've actually created a scene here. The food is a nice touch. Of course, it's hardly original."

Ellis put his gun hand down on the table but kept his finger on the trigger. He'd miss me, barely, if he fired from that position. I still wasn't in a spot to do anything about it, though. "It doesn't need to be original," he said. "The original was incomplete. Unfinished. This one won't be." He nodded at the plate in front of me. "You should try the steak."

"I already ate," I said. "If I'd known you were making steak, I might have waited."

Sarah tried to say something but it was muffled by the tape. Ellis glanced at her. "I think Sarah would like some," he said. He looked back at me. "I can't feed her and hold the gun, obviously, but if you want to give her something, I won't stop you."

"I think what she was saying was you should get up and run away from here as fast as you possibly can."

Ellis smirked. "Why? You going to kill me, Nevada?" He tapped the barrel of his gun on the table. "I don't think you've thought about how this ends."

"It's pretty obvious you haven't, either," I said. "How are you going to explain this? Are you going to say you found us here, dead, and you have no idea what happened? This is some haphazard shit you've got going on here."

He nodded. "That's true. I had to advance my timeline much faster than I wanted to. I'd thought I'd have time to play with you for a while, just to show *him* I could do it better. But Sarah here…" he frowned at her. "Sarah started asking questions. She was pretty subtle at first, but then someone in the department told me she ran the GPS on my car to see where I'd been going." He shook his head at her. "I'm not stupid enough to have used my own car," he said, "but the fact that you were asking was trouble enough."

I shifted my left arm, just enough to give me better access to my Glock. I was fast, but not enough to clear the shoulder holster and get a shot off before he put a bullet in me. Drawing from a seated position was going to be awkward, anyway. It would add time I didn't have to waste getting into position. Even if he took his hand off his gun he'd be able to recover it and get a shot off before I could. "You haven't explained how you're not going to get caught."

"I've got some experience rigging crime scenes now," he said. "I think I'll manage."

I shrugged. "You should still run. I promise I'll give you five minutes before I start chasing you. How about that?"

Ellis stared at me. "How are you so calm?" he asked. "Did you…" he glanced around the room. "No. Nobody's coming. If you had a SWAT team on the way they'd have kicked in the door by now. You act like you knew it was me and none of this is a surprise, though."

"I didn't know it was you," I said. "My money was on someone in law enforcement, though. I kept going out there and critiquing crime scenes. The killer was learning from me. You thought it was about the blood and the bodies, but that was never right. It was about art. It was about the meaning he left behind."

Ellis nodded. "I did catch on."

Sarah said something else and struggled against the tape that held her in place. Trying to distract him, I thought. Clever girl. If she could goad him into taking his attention off of me long enough, maybe I could do something. He'd never fall for it, though. He'd kill her first.

"It took a shift in my thinking," Ellis said. "I didn't get it at first, but now I do. But it's also about the game."

"Which is why I'm here? Why you sent me flowers? That was a nice touch, by the way, but I knew they weren't from the Laughing Man."

"No," he said. "You weren't supposed to. The game isn't about me being the Laughing Man. It's about me succeeding him. The student becomes the master. The game is the game, and we are the players."

"If Buddha cuts a tree down…" I started. "Wait, that's wrong. Give me a second. I've got one. If the bear shits in the forest, is he also the Pope?"

Ellis blinked. "What?"

"Oh, I'm sorry," I said "I thought we were having a contest to say a bunch of stupid nonsense. 'The game is the game?' What the fuck does that even mean?"

"It means I'm playing with him, not you. We're the kings. White and black, sitting across the board from each other."

"Am I a queen, then? Or how about a bishop? I always liked bishops."

He shook his head. "No. You're just a trophy."

"That's no fun," I said. "But anyway, somehow I think you're the only one playing this game. You think the Laughing Man gives two shits about you? You're just a pretender."

"That won't be true once you're dead. Then he'll play with me. I'll be the only one *worth* playing with. I'll have proved it."

I thought about that. "I guess I can kind of see what you're getting at," I said.

"And what do you think?"

"Honestly?" I asked. "I wonder what happened to you." I shook my head. "Dan said you were in a shoot a while back and you barely got through your psych evaluation after. Was that it? Was that what set you off, or are you the type of psycho who set fires and wet the bed when you were a kid?"

Ellis reached into a pocket and removed a folded straight razor. He snapped it open and admired the blade. "It was the shoot," he said. "That's what did it. It was…transformative." He sighed. "You've killed, Nevada. I know you have."

"Yes."

He looked at me, eyes wide. "What was it like for you? The first time?"

My first shoot had been a killer who had holed up in his bedroom and come out shooting when I tried to talk him down. Everything about it had been clean, but… "It made me sick," I said. "I cried for a week." I shook my head. "I still see him sometimes. In crowds. Just for a second. I'll look again and he's gone."

Ellis looked at me like I'd just told him I hated ice cream and puppies. "Really?"

"Really. Let me guess. Yours made you feel alive for the first time. It filled you with...I don't know. Power? Sex stuff? If you tell me you came in your pants I'll come over this table at you, I swear to god."

"Nothing like that," he said. "It was power, Nevada. Just the power."

"I almost feel sorry for you," I said. "Almost. Not enough that I won't blow your head off if I get the chance."

Ellis fingered the straight razor. "I'd love to use this on you while you're still alive," he said. "I really wonder what that would be like. But it would be breaking the rules, of course. The game is nothing without rules."

I sighed. "The game again. But you screwed up, you know? You made a mistake."

"Oh? I don't see how."

"You know the Laughing Man is watching me. He's obsessed, you could say. You know what he did with the last guy who tried to off me." Ellis squinted at me. "Walked up behind him and cut his throat right when he was in the gloating stage. What makes you think..." I took my eyes off of him and fixed my gaze on the spot over his right shoulder.

Ellis turned his head to look behind him, which took his gun even farther off of me than it had been before. That was all I needed. In the time it took him to realize nobody was coming and look back I had my Glock out of its holster and pointed at his head. "That wasn't the mistake," I said. "The mistake was not knowing I'm a Glock girl."

Ellis stared at my gun, then his eyes drifted down to look at his own. He wasn't in position to shoot. "Don't do it," I said. "Even if you manage to get a shot off, I'll drop you. Put it down."

Sarah said something that sounded very much like "Ha!" through the tape covering her mouth.

Ellis looked at his gun for a moment longer, then slowly lowered it onto the table and took his hand away. "You're right," he said. "You got me."

"Put your hands flat on..." I started, but Ellis shoved the table at me instead, knocking it into me and sending me flying backward in a waterfall of plates and food. I got off one shot in his direction as I fell to the ground, but it went wide. He was gone an instant later, running for the front door. I heard it open as I got to my feet. "Damn it!" I shouted. I braced to go after him but Sarah started screaming something through her tape, shaking her head wildly. She was right. As much as my instincts wanted me to go after Ellis, it was too dangerous. He could be waiting in the bushes for me to come out, and he still had my .45, and probably his service weapon, as well. Plus it would mean leaving Sarah here defenseless, and there was no help on the way if something happened to me.

I pulled the tape off her mouth. "My god, Nevada," she said. "I'm so sorry. I should have..."

"Forget it," I said. I took a steak knife from off of the floor in one hand, keeping my Glock at the ready in the other, and went to work on the tape that bound her to the chair. The minute she was free I started looking for a phone, finding one in the kitchen. Thankfully, it had a dial tone. "It's over," I told Sarah. "We'll wait here until SWAT comes. That asshole won't get far."

Chapter 20

The first uniforms arrived six minutes later and secured the scene. Then the detectives came to do their thing, and shortly after Dan Evans arrived to do *his* thing. His thing involved a great deal of cursing and slamming his fist into the wall hard enough to put cracks in it. Sarah and I gave statements. Sarah had been onto Ellis fairly early. If I hadn't been ignoring her messages it was possible none of this would have happened. I didn't feel great about that.

After a while I told Dan I needed to step out and get some air. Part of that was the truth. The air outside was cool and it did help clear my head. And then I got in my Mustang and headed for Miramar.

Dan called five minutes later. "Where the *hell* are you, Nevada?"

"I was done," I told him. "You think I need half the department following me home? The last time this happened you had me under surveillance for a month."

"That was to protect you, you dumb shit."

"Yeah, I know. It was pretty annoying, though."

"Where are you, Nevada?"

"I'm not telling."

He swore for a while. When he was done I said, "Take Sarah to the hospital and make sure someone stays with her. She's going to blame herself, but none of this is her fault. Make sure she understands that."

"It's not her fault," Dan said. "It's my fault. The son of a bitch was right under my nose."

"Psychopaths are hard to spot, Dan. That's why they're called psychopaths." I thought about that statement. "Well, no, that's not really why they're called psychopaths. The word origin is...not really relevant, I guess. The point is you couldn't have seen this coming."

"I'm going to tear him apart if I ever get my hands on him. I'm serious, Nevada."

I sighed. Dan was the most upstanding, honest cop I'd ever met, but Ellis made the second person I had no doubt he'd execute without so much as an arrest or trial. The Laughing Man was the other one. Spending time around me really wasn't a healthy thing. "Get some rest, Dan. And put a new team on it. No, screw that. Call in another department. SDPD Homicide is going to be pretty shaken up. I don't think your people are going to be at their best."

"We'll find him," Dan said. "I promise you that, Nevada. We'll find him."

"I know."

"Now where are you?"

"In the wind," I said.

"What the hell does…" he started, but I hung up on him. When the phone started to ring again, I shut the power off. I wasn't in the mood for conversation.

I drove all the way to my motel in Miramar and sat in the Mustang for a good ten minutes, trying to decide what to do next. Drinking had never sounded as good as it did right now. I still had vodka in my room. I'd brought my security bottle with me when I'd hastily moved up here. But another part of me, a surprisingly strong part, didn't want the drink. It wanted to go to the roof of a tall building to shout and scream at the sky. Ideally it would be raining when I did this; it would have been good for dramatic effect, but it had been a clear day and rain hadn't been in the forecast.

I powered my cell phone back on and looked through the voicemail, erasing the messages Dan had left without listening to them. There was very little doubt as to their content. It would be all swearing and demands that I go somewhere he could make sure I was safe.

As strange as it might have sounded, the only person I really wanted to call right now was the one person I had no way of reaching. The Laughing Man. It was sick, but he was really the only other person on Earth capable of understanding any of this. In another very, very strange world, we might have been friends.

Eventually I gave up and went into my room. The vodka I'd brought along was still in my suitcase. I took the bottle and turned the television on, then sat on the bed to watch it. The truth was I had no interest in the TV. I just wanted to hold the liquor. It was my old friend. It would keep me safe.

Halfway through some late-night talk show I realized I was shaking. Was that adrenaline, or was it the vodka in my hand? I hadn't opened the bottle yet. It was about three-quarters full. It would be enough to knock me out if I could get the whole thing down without vomiting. That itself would be a test. In the last of my drinking days my body hadn't reacted well to alcohol at all. If I wasn't already drunk I'd had to fight to keep the first few swallows from coming back up.

I opened the bottle, sniffed the contents, and gagged almost immediately. With my eyes and mouth watering, I closed the bottle. Not yet. I wasn't going to drink it yet.

The phone rang and I ignored it, not even bothering to check the caller ID this time. The late-night show ended and an infomercial started up. The guy was hawking an amazing secret for cleaning dirty clothes. It seemed to involve some kind of spray. Also, if you ordered quickly enough, you could get three bottles for the price of one, and you could pay for them in small installments. I wondered if you could just pay them everything up front. Probably. It didn't seem worth calling to check. When I did laundry, I just used the cheapest detergent from the store. It seemed to work just fine.

I turned the cap on the vodka again. Smelled it. My mouth started watering, but I didn't gag this time. I screwed the bottle shut. My hands were shaking again. Now I knew it was the alcohol. The adrenaline had worn off a long time ago.

I put the vodka down on the nightstand and took my Glock out of its holster. I'd been asked to surrender it as evidence, but I'd told Dan anyone who tried to take it from me was going to get a bullet in the neck. Brad Ellis still had my .45 and

I wasn't going anywhere unarmed. God only knew what Ellis had done with the other gun. Maybe he'd blown his dick off while he'd been running away with it in his pants. That would have been fitting.

The Glock still had the powder smell on it from its recent firing. On another day I'd have taken it apart and cleaned it, but that would have meant leaving myself unarmed. There was no way in hell that was going to happen anytime in the near future. Maybe I'd ask Dan for another gun so I had a backup piece. Or maybe I'd just get my own. The more guns I had that he didn't know about, the better. That would make it harder for him to take them away from me if he ever decided to try.

I dropped the magazine on the Glock into my palm, looked it over, and slid it back into place. I could have popped another bullet into it, but that didn't seem that important. I had plenty left. If Brad Ellis had any sense at all he wasn't coming after me. He would be halfway to Los Angeles by now. Or he could have gone to Mexico. They didn't even check IDs when you entered from the U.S. Nobody cared about who you were until you tried to come back. Did Ellis speak Spanish? That might be worth asking, but someone else could ask it. I was done with this.

For a moment I had an urge to turn the gun on myself and pull the trigger. Everything would be over in a split second. I'd never have to worry about anything again. It probably wouldn't even hurt.

I sighed, put the Glock down, and picked the vodka up again. The bottle seemed heavier now. It couldn't be, of course. My mind was playing tricks on me. The clear liquid inside looked appealing. It wasn't expensive stuff and this brand tasted more like industrial chemicals than anything a person should actually drink, but it would get the job done. There was no doubt about that. If I managed to get it down I wouldn't wake up until tomorrow afternoon. Sleep would be nice. And booze chased away the nightmares, if I drank enough of it. I knew that from experience.

The cap was off the bottle almost before I noticed my hands were unscrewing it again. Once again the smell hit me hard, but I didn't gag this time. That probably wasn't a good thing. It was becoming familiar now. My body was getting used to it again.

I glared at the bottle, then raised it and took a good-sized sip into my mouth. The liquid didn't feel like anything more than water in my mouth, but it wouldn't as long as I was holding my breath. So what if I swallowed it? What was it going to matter?

Then I turned my head and spat it onto the motel carpet. My mouth and nasal passages started burning from the liquid almost immediately. I gagged once, then went to the sink and gagged again. I put the bottle down and rinsed my mouth out with tap water. If any of the vodka had made it down my throat, I couldn't feel it. I'd probably be smelling it for a while, though.

I picked up the bottle and took a long look at it, then turned it over and poured the contents into the sink, watching as the liquid swirled and disappeared down the drain. When it was gone I ran the sink for a few minutes to flush it away. Then I capped the bottle and tossed it into the trash can. I wasn't going to be drinking tonight. Maybe someday I would, if I got low enough. But it wouldn't be tonight. And it wouldn't be because I had a bad day. Or at least, it would have to be a worse day than this had been.

I went back to the bed and looked for something else to watch on television. It was a reasonable bet that I wasn't going to sleep tonight.

Chapter 21

"You look like shit," Dan said the next morning as he sat down.

I'd been toying with the second half of my Denver omelet, pushing bits of it around my plate like race cars around a track, when he arrived. I'd told him to meet me at a Denny's when I finally returned one of his calls. I didn't feel like going down to the station, which is where I knew he wanted me.

"I didn't get much sleep," I said.

"That's not really a surprise." He asked for a cup of coffee as the waitress passed by. "You don't smell like booze, though. I was wondering if I was going to have to drag your ass to detox."

"To be honest, so was I. How's Sarah?"

Dan shrugged. "Shaken up but she's taking it better than I would have expected. I think I underestimated her. She's more angry at herself than anything else. Thinks she should have acted faster when she started to suspect Ellis."

"Nobody wants to point the finger at another cop," I said. "Her career would have been over if she'd been wrong. Hell, it might have been over even if she was right." I speared a piece of ham, but wasn't hungry enough to put it in my mouth. "She reached out to me but I ignored her because I didn't want to deal with it. That's on me."

"Yeah. That is on you."

I blinked. That hadn't exactly been what I'd expected to hear. "You do remember I'm not a cop anymore, right?"

"I seem to remember telling you a while back you're always going to be a cop," he said. "That doesn't change because you're not wearing the badge." He pointed at me. "You have responsibilities. To me. To Sarah. To the department."

I looked at him. "You know what? You're right about you and Sarah. I haven't done some of the things I should have."

"No, you certainly..." he started.

I cut him off. "But fuck the department. I don't care about the department anymore. Did you bring my badge along with you?" He nodded. "Throw it in the trash. I'm never putting it back on."

Dan pursed his lips and watched as I took a drink of my Diet Coke. "Your poker face needs work," he said.

"What?"

"You're not upset at the department. It's something else. Is it that you think you should have spotted Ellis, too? Are you mad at yourself?"

"I'm just mad," I said.

"What's going on, Nevada?"

177

I sighed. Meeting him in person had been a mistake. "I've been working on something else," I admitted. "Privately."

His eyes widened. "You have another case? Tell me it's not organized crime again."

"No. Odds are you'll hear the details soon enough. It's just…I thought I was doing the right thing. I thought I was going to help an old lady find some closure for something she went through a long time ago. And I've realized that if what I think happened is what happened, then no good is going to come out of it whatsoever. If I do everything by the book, a guy who made a terrible mistake twenty years ago is going to prison for the rest of his life. I should drop the whole thing and move to Tahiti."

"If I thought you'd stay there, I'd buy you the ticket myself." He sighed. "But you'd get bored, Nevada. You always get bored."

"Yeah." I pushed my plate aside. I wasn't going to be eating any more. "I just wonder what the point of all this is."

The waitress came to refill Dan's coffee and this time left the pot. He took a sip and grimaced. "You know this isn't the first time we've had this conversation."

"Oh?"

"Maybe you don't remember. Marjorie Hamlin. This was…seven years ago? I was still a sergeant."

I let the name bounce around my head. "Older woman. Shoved her husband during an argument?"

Dan nodded. "He fell down and hit his head wrong. Got a bleed on the brain and died three days later. We had no history of abuse on either side, no previous incidents. By all accounts it was just a terrible accident."

"Yeah."

"She was looking at a homicide charge. Got scared. You brought her in when she ran and then you started yelling at me."

"That sounds like something I'd do."

"You asked what the point was. She was an old lady, she hadn't meant to kill anyone, she was no danger to anyone else. She had to live with what she'd done. What was the point of putting her in prison? Wasn't the pain of living with what she'd done bad enough?"

"And what did you say, o wise one?"

"You know exactly what I said."

"Tell me anyway. I think I need to hear it."

He nodded. "I said *we* weren't putting her in prison. We were bringing her in so justice could be served. What form that took was for the court to decide. She had to stand in front of a jury and put the decision to them. Twelve people would hear what happened, look at the evidence, and then decide what needed to be done." He reached across the table and took one of my hands. "Because there has to be an accounting, Nevada. People need to be accountable for what they've done. And as I remember it, Marjorie Hamlin got probation."

"That sounds about right," I said.

"So whatever this thing is that you're not telling me about, keep in mind that you aren't judge, jury and executioner. That's not your role. You don't decide right and wrong. You're just an agent that gives justice the opportunity to be served."

I leaned back. "Look at you dropping philosophy," I said. "When did you get so eloquent?"

He shrugged. "Sometimes I want to grab you and shake you, Nevada, but that wouldn't get me far. I do this instead."

"Thanks," I said. "I actually feel a little better."

"Good."

"I'm still putting a bullet in the Laughing Man when I catch up with him, though."

"Not if I beat you to it." He smiled faintly. "I'm going to wait a couple days, and then we're going to have another conversation about your badge."

"My answer isn't going to be different. Maybe don't throw it in the trash, though. I worked hard to get it."

"It suits you. Also, I like it when you have to follow my orders."

"I never followed your orders."

He shrugged. "Fair enough. I like it when I can keep an eye on you, then. You want to tell me where you've been staying?"

"It doesn't matter. I'll be moving back to my old motel soon. You should come over. We'll get a pizza and watch awful television."

He nodded. "Deal. Anyway, I've got to go. My guys are having a pretty bad day and I should be there, but I needed to see you first. Good luck with this thing you're doing. Let me know how it works out."

On impulse, I stuck my hand out and he shook it. That wasn't something we did very often. Later, I'd wonder what had been going on in my head to make me want to do that. Maybe it was the thought that everything was going to be okay.

Chapter 22

Del Mar was just up the coast. I could have called ahead but I didn't think this was going to be a long conversation, and even though I doubted Conrad Meyers was going to run, I'd have looked like an idiot if he did.

His house was easy to find. It was in a modest suburb in the hills overlooking the ocean. I couldn't think of the last time I'd been up here. I doubted I'd been looking for a murder suspect at the time. Del Mar wasn't exactly a hotbed of violent crime. It was more a hotbed of BMWs and overpriced restaurants.

I parked on the street and sat in the car watching the house for a while. My Glock was tucked away in its shoulder holster. I doubted I was going to need it here.

After a few minutes of thinking it over, I got out and went up to the front door to ring the bell. A man in his late forties opened it. He had graying hair and wore a green cardigan. My first thought was that I should tell him to lose the cardigan. He looked like he was about to audition for a new version of the

Mister Rogers show.

He smiled at me. "I'd be happy to take a brochure, miss."

I blinked. "What?"

"Oh," he said. "I thought you must be a Jehovah's Witness. They come by sometimes to hand out their literature."

"No," I shook my head. "My name is Nevada James. I used to be with the San Diego Police Department. Are you Conrad Meyers?"

"I am," he said. He squinted his eyes slightly. "I think I've seen you on television. You were at a crime scene."

And they said people didn't watch local news anymore. "That was me," I admitted.

"You can't think I know something about that? I don't. Did you want to come inside?" He moved aside so I could have entered. I didn't really want to.

"No," I said. "I'm here about something else." I stuck my hands in my pockets. "I'm here to ask you about the Adam Collins bombing from 1993. I was wondering if..."

There was no need to finish the sentence. Conrad's face had gone white. And then the bastard started to cry.

***

I called Anita Collins two hours later as I was driving back to San Diego. "It's over," I said. "I found the bomber."

In the background I could hear voices in conversation and clinking sounds that must have been glasses knocking together. I hadn't bothered to ask where she was. It seemed early for a cocktail party. Maybe she was at a brunch.

For a long time she didn't say anything. "Anita?" I asked.

"I'm here," she said. "Sorry. That really wasn't what I was expecting to hear this morning."

"Are you busy? You sound like you're at a party. I could call back, I guess."

"Nothing is more important than this," she said. I heard her take a deep breath. "Tell me."

Traffic was light heading back into San Diego, but I put her on speaker so I could keep my hands on the wheel. "His name is Conrad Meyers. He was getting his Ph.D. when he became aware of your husband's work."

"I've heard the name. As I remember...he was the one my donor brought to me. He developed that treatment for malaria everyone was raving about."

"Yeah."

She snorted. "Was that supposed to be some kind of joke? Coming to me like that after he'd killed my family?"

"No," I said. "It was supposed to be penance."

"I see. Penance." She was silent again. I waited. I didn't imagine this was easy to hear. "Explain it to me."

"Your husband worked in artificial intelligence. Meyers was an anti-technology...I guess *zealot* is the word I'm looking for, but that hardly jibes with the guy I just met. Anyway, he believed, or at least he believed at the time, that computers were going to lead to the breakdown of human society. It was the beginning of the Internet age. The world was changing. He thought computers doing our thinking for us was going to be the beginning of the end."

Anita snorted. "Was he twelve years old? What kind of stupid..." She stopped for a moment. "And he thought my husband deserved to die for this?"

"No. The bomb...it wasn't supposed to do what it did. He'd been working with, and forgive me if I don't get all of this right, oxide chains, or something about oxide chains and peroxide bonds...I probably should have written this down. Anyway, he thought the bomb was going to make a big *bang* and smoke like crazy. After the note he left, he thought that would be frightening enough to make your husband give up his work. Meyers said he had no idea the explosion would be as powerful as it was. Nobody was supposed to get hurt."

"And yet my husband and child are dead, and I look like..." She stopped. "All that for nothing."

I opened my mouth but realized I was about to defend Meyers, which wasn't what I meant to do at all. Maybe all the crying had gotten to me. Sitting in his living room while he cried on his couch, and then his wife cried, and when they called their son at his college to tell him what was happening...it had been a long, unpleasant morning. I didn't care to repeat the experience anytime soon. The next time someone asked me to look at a cold case, I was going to tell them to get stuffed.

"What happens now?" Anita asked. "Where is he?"

"I gave him a day to put his house in order," I said. "He's turning himself in tomorrow. They'll charge him with whatever they decide is appropriate."

"You let him go?"

"He's not going to run. In his mind he's been running for

twenty years. I think part of him was relieved to finally be caught."

"How nice for him."

"Anyway, that's where we stand. I figured you'd want to know. I'm done with this now."

Now I was fairly certain I could hear a string quartet playing somewhere near Anita. It sounded like I was missing quite a party. Well, it probably wasn't the kind of party I'd be interested in, except for the free food. Although I wasn't hungry. I doubted I would be again for a while. The whole experience with Meyers had left me feeling nauseous.

"I'm sorry," Anita said. "I should sound grateful, and I am. It's just…"

"I wasn't offended. I'm not going to say I know what you're going through, but I'm sure it's not easy."

"It's not," she said. "But after all this time, I'm grateful it's almost over. The truth is I didn't expect you to be successful. Come by the house later and we'll talk about your compensation."

"Nah," I said. "I don't really care. All things considered it wasn't much work, and I still have Alan Davies's money burning a hole in my pocket."

"I have to give you something."

"I'll call you in a few days," I said. "Right now I think I need a vacation."

Chapter 23

I didn't take a vacation. I probably should have, but sitting on a beach by myself didn't sound all that appealing. Besides, if I wanted to sit on the beach, it was only a ten minute drive away from anywhere in the city. San Diego was good that way.

A week passed with no sign of Brad Ellis. I doubted he was still in California. Mexico seemed more and more likely. These days it was harder and harder to get around in the U.S. without a camera getting a shot of your face. If facial recognition didn't get him, someone would notice him sooner or later. He'd been the biggest story on the nightly news since the night he'd revealed himself. There had even been national coverage. I doubted he'd have wanted to stick around.

The second biggest story in San Diego had been Conrad Meyers, who had been true to his word and walked into SDPD headquarters with his wife and his lawyer the day after I'd visited him. There was a great deal of talk about the Unabomber and how the crimes had been similar, some even speculating that Meyers had hoped the other man's *modus operandi* had been close enough that his attack would be confused for the Unabomber's work. They were right about that. Meyers had told me so himself. He had been a copycat, after all.

I called Harold Lanford's house a few hours after Meyers turned himself in. Julia answered the phone. "It's Nevada James here," I said. "Is Detective Lanford up?"

Julia sniffed. "Detective James," she said. From her voice I could tell she'd been crying. "Howard...Detective Lanford..." She didn't need to finish the sentence. My heart sank.

"Damn it," I said. "I'm too late."

Julia started crying again. I was starting to get sick of people crying every time I opened my mouth. "I'm sorry," I said.

"No," she said. "It meant a lot to him that you came to talk to him. He said it made him feel useful again."

"That's nice to hear. He helped me a lot. I wish I could have told him."

One more thing I'd get to regret for the rest of my life. At least this one wasn't technically my fault.

Over the course of the week I spent a few afternoons working out in Molly Malone's dojo, moved back into my old motel in Mission Valley, and made an effort to be somewhat social. Dan Evans came out and took another statement from me. I met Sarah Winters for coffee. She looked like shit, but she'd survive. Sarah was an almost stupidly nice person and I still thought she ought to reconsider her life choices and become a kindergarten teacher. She could be a warrior when she needed to be, though. After what had happened with Ellis, she was going to be a lot harder to fool in the future.

Part of me wondered if that was a good or a bad thing. She'd never really get over what had happened. Nobody ever did. There was something about me that had liked her continual optimism. Or was it innocence? Maybe. And maybe I'd just been underestimating her again.

I spent an hour one afternoon looking at what was quickly becoming my new house in Ocean Beach. It was coming along well. I'd probably be able to move in by the end of the month. I was looking forward to having my own place again. Nearly everything I owned was in storage, including my motorcycle. It wasn't like I owned a huge number of things, but it would be nice to see the things I *did* have once in a while.

Once I was back in my old motel I thought about buying another bottle of vodka to keep nearby in case I needed to hold it, but ultimately decided against it. I wasn't sure I needed it anymore. That might change, but for the time being I seemed to be all right without it. Progress, I guess. I even went to an A.A. meeting and told everyone about it. Half of them looked at me like I was crazy. The other half understood. A.A. was always like that.

Anita Collins did a half-hour interview on one of the morning news shows. They went to her house to film her in the room with the paintings of her family. She was in her kindly grandmother mode, smiling fondly as she recalled her husband and son. "It's been a long wait, but justice will finally be served," she said. My name wasn't mentioned. That was by design. As far as anyone in the media knew, I had nothing to do with any of this. The last thing I needed was a gaggle of reporters outside my motel door.

I went down to the pier at Ocean Beach one afternoon and bought a box of lobster tacos and fries. I gave about half of the fries to a group of excited seagulls while I watched the waves roll in. Later I wondered if it was okay for seagulls to eat fries. Probably. Unless seagulls were susceptible to heart disease. Then it wouldn't be so great.

The next day I was watching *The Price is Right* in my motel when the news broke in. Conrad Meyers was being arraigned and was going to be making a statement to the media on the courthouse steps. I'd been told a deal was in the works; he was going to plead down to two counts of manslaughter. He was still probably going to spend the rest of his life in prison, unless he got a heck of a lot of time off for good behavior. He didn't seem like the type who was going to be starting shit with the guards or joining a gang in prison, so that seemed like a possibility.

I went outside to get some fresh ice and two cans of Diet Coke from the motel's vending machine. When I got back Conrad's lawyer was speaking. I turned the volume down. I didn't need to listen to it. Conrad stood next to the lawyer, eyes on the ground, nodding now and again. He looked a great deal weaker than when I'd seen him last. That wasn't a surprise. I didn't feel good about sending him to prison, but like Dan had said, it wasn't me sending him, anyway. Two people were dead, whether he'd meant to kill them or not. There had to be an accounting for that. What it wound up being wasn't for me to say.

After a moment Conrad's lawyer turned to him and nodded. Conrad stepped forward and looked out at the assembled media. I didn't need the volume to understand what he was saying. The apology he was giving was written all over his face.

There was a sudden commotion and the camera turned

away from Meyers as if someone had bumped into the cameraman. When it found Meyers again Anita Collins was with him. She'd worn a black suit that looked like it belonged at a funeral. Where had she come from? Had she been asked to make a statement? If that was the case, it wouldn't be at *this* press conference. Unless she was going to announce she was forgiving him, but I'd have bet good money that wasn't going to happen.

Anita put one hand on Meyers's chest and said something to him. She had a gentle smile on her face. Maybe she was going to forgive him, after all. Then her other hand went into her purse. I saw it emerge with the knife at the same time Meyers did, just before she drove it into his chest. Meyers staggered and the camera moved; people were panicking now, trying to get away. When it came back to the podium Anita had removed the knife and was driving it into Meyers again. She got a third stab in before a police officer managed to grab her around the waist and pull her away.

The camera lingered on Meyers's body for a moment before the feed cut out and then switched back to the studio, where the two anchors looked like they had no idea what to do. One of them was moving his mouth but I'd never turned the volume up so I couldn't tell what he was saying. It didn't matter much. Meyers had taken three good hits in the chest, from what I'd seen. If he was still alive at all, he wouldn't be for long.

I was an idiot. Anita had told me it was *almost* over. She'd told the press that justice *would be* served. I'd thought she was talking about the trial that was coming. She hadn't been. She'd never planned for there to be a trial. If I'd listened to her back when I'd been at her house I might have realized the truth.

This was always going to end in blood.

Chapter 24

I drove out to Playa del Mar a week later. I could have gone earlier, but I'd put it off until I thought I'd be able to do this and stay reasonably calm.

The security guard out front was the same guy I'd talked to before. He didn't greet me when I stopped. He nodded once, then opened the gate without a word. He looked like someone had shot his dog.

Two minutes passed from when I rang the bell to when Anita opened her front door. She wore sweat pants and an old t-shirt that left the scars on her left arm fully exposed. My eyes lingered on them a second longer than they should have. I wondered what they felt like.

Anita shrugged. "Come in." She didn't bother with any of her grandma routine today. That was just as well. I'd have been tempted to shoot her if she pulled that shit with me.

I stepped inside and she shut the door. "I was surprised they didn't keep you locked up," I said.

Anita tugged on the right leg of her sweat pants and showed me the ankle monitor she was wearing. "I'm not exactly a flight risk. Even this seemed excessive, if you ask me."

"Yeah."

"Do you want tea? Coffee?"

"No," I said. "I want to punch you in your fucking face."

She nodded. "You can if you want. I don't really care. Let's go sit."

Anita led me into the room full of paintings where we'd met before. It looked the same as it had last time, except she'd lit more than a dozen candles around the room. Classical music was playing from a speaker in the corner. I was fairly certain it was Vivaldi. "Is this *Four Seasons*?"

"Yes," she said. "Adam liked it." She nodded at a couch. "Sit, Nevada. We may as well get this over with."

I sat on one of her blue couches and she sat down across from me. A half full glass of white wine sat on the table between us. She picked it up and took a sip, closing her eyes as she savored the taste. "This is a Stonestreet chardonnay," she said. "It's wonderful. I hope you don't think me rude that I don't offer you a glass. I heard you've got nearly four months of sobriety now." She peered at me. "Or have you relapsed? If that's the case…" she held up the glass.

"No," I said. "I haven't relapsed."

"Congratulations, then."

"I didn't come here for congratulations."

"No," she said. "You came here to be angry with me. Fine.

194

Be angry. I honestly don't care, Nevada."

Part of me wanted to grab her and shake her. "You lied to me."

She shrugged. "I told you what you needed to hear. You were going on about the *system*, and if I'd told you what I was planning you would have walked out the door." She looked at me with eyes of steel. "I was always going to kill him, Nevada. It's all I've wanted for twenty years."

I wasn't sure what to say to her that was going to get through. "Do you think this is what your family would have wanted?"

"I don't know." She looked over at a portrait of her husband. "Adam was a gentle man. He would have said violence was never the answer. But he also didn't know he and his son would die because some deluded hippie was afraid computers would take over the world." She shrugged. "Anyway, it doesn't matter. It was what *I* wanted." The corner of her mouth turned upward into a crooked smile. "I think you probably don't want to hear a thank you, but I'll say it anyway. Thank you, Nevada. I truly didn't think you'd be able to find him for me. You were my last hope. And you came through." She raised her glass in a toast. "Cheers."

"He wasn't…" I started. "He wasn't a bad man. He did something stupid and it had tragic consequences, but it wasn't an act of evil."

"It's strange to hear you defend him," Anita said. "But here's the simple truth, Nevada." She leaned forward and looked into my eyes. "I don't care."

I'd never been a wine drinker but a glass of something

strong didn't sound half bad right now. "You're going to go to prison."

"I doubt it," she said. "Maybe. But I also have trouble believing a jury is going to put this," she scrunched up her face and became the kindly grandmother, "*nice old lady* in jail." She relaxed and grandma was gone. "Maybe they will. But I don't care. My life ended twenty years ago. If I spend a few years in a cell..." she looked around. "This will still be here when I get back. And if I never come back...if I die behind bars, I'll *still* have killed the man who murdered my family. I win."

I sat on the couch, trying to think of something clever to say. The truth was I'd been outplayed. I'd seen through her old lady act, so she showed me her real face. Apparently I'd been so impressed it had made me unable to see what was really going on.

"Anyway," she said. "Don't you think you're being a bit hypocritical?"

"How?"

"You're trying to tell me I did the wrong thing, but the truth is you're going to do exactly what I did when you catch up with the Laughing Man." I tensed up, ready to say something nasty, but the words failed me. "You're not going to trust your precious system to deal with him, Nevada. You told me yourself you're going to kill him. As slowly as you can. That's what you said. You need for it to hurt. Tell me I'm wrong, Nevada. Have you reconsidered all of that since the last time you sat in this room?"

I supposed we were past the point of lies. "No," I said. "I haven't."

"Then you'll have to forgive me for thinking I'm entitled to the same justice you are." She smiled. "Now, if you're not going to have a drink, I think you should leave. This conversation is getting tedious."

I stood up and headed for the door. Just before leaving the room I turned. "Let me ask you something?"

She nodded. "You may."

It was an awful thing to ask, but there were only so many people I could put this question to. "What did it feel like? When you killed him? After all that time?"

Anita gave me an appraising look and sipped her wine. "Because it's you, I'll answer that." She looked me in the eyes. "It felt *wonderful*, Nevada. It felt..." she sighed. "It felt so good. The release of all that pain... It may have been the best thing I've ever done."

I considered that. "Yeah," I said. "That's about what I thought." Then I turned and left. I didn't look back.

Chapter 25

My motel room phone rang at two in the morning. I hadn't heard it in so long that at first I thought it was some kind of demented alarm clock rousing me out of sleep. When I was conscious enough to stop hitting the handset like a snooze button, I picked it up. "Yeah?"

"Ma'am?" a man's voice asked. "This is the front desk. I'm sorry to bother you at this hour, but you have a caller asking to be transferred over. He said it's an emergency."

I took a deep breath. There was little question about who this was going to be. "Do you have caller ID on that phone?"

"It says the number is blocked."

"Fine," I said. "Put him through."

There was a clicking noise and then I heard the sound of the caller breathing through his mask. Somehow I wasn't surprised he'd wear it even for just a phone call. "Hello, Nevada," the Laughing Man said.

His voice was a tenor, musical, and just slightly distorted by the mask. "It's a little late," I told him. "Or early, I guess. Whichever."

He was silent for a long moment. I might have thought he'd hung up if not for his audible breathing. "You still there?" I asked.

"I need to be very clear with you about this," the Laughing Man said. "This is not part of our game. This was a personal matter that had to be taken care of."

"Yeah. I get that."

"He was…an imitator, and a poor one at that. His work was an obscenity. I couldn't allow it to stand."

I didn't need to ask what he was talking about. I knew what he'd done. "You don't have to explain it to me," I said. "I'm not going to lose any sleep over it."

"Good. I'm glad. You need your sleep. Sleep keeps the mind sharp, and I like you better when your mind is sharp."

I sighed. "Let me ask you something?"

"Of course."

I hesitated, not sure how to word the question. "Why haven't you started the game yet? Back in my house you told me how much you'd missed it, but that was three months ago and you've done nothing. I was starting to think I wouldn't hear from you again."

"No," the Laughing Man said. "Not at all. It's just that we can only play once. It will be our last game. When it is over, at least one of us will be dead. So the stakes are quite high, you see?"

"Are you afraid of me?"

He chuckled. "Maybe a little. I don't long for death, and you're certainly capable of killing me. But that wasn't what I meant. If we can only play once, don't you think it's important that we should have a very *good* game?"

"I don't think I can answer that without sounding like a sociopath."

"No? Tell me you wouldn't be disappointed if I walked into the police station right now and turned myself in."

"I *would* be disappointed," I said. "It would mean I don't get to shoot you."

"And it would mean I don't get to put you in a still life. What a waste that would be. I've had some very interesting ideas along those lines."

"I'm sure you have."

"Anyway, I should be going. This is a burner phone and as much as I'm sure you're not tracing me, I'd have to be stupid to take the chance."

"Aw," I said. "I was hoping we'd have some time to catch up. Talk about old times."

"Believe it or not, I'd like that, too. There really is nobody else who would understand. But I'll have to pass. Tonight, anyway. Maybe not the next time we talk."

"I'm looking forward to it," I said. "Anyway, you know I'm not getting out of bed to go look for the body. You called to give me a location so I could go see it. Tell me where it is."

He chuckled, gave me an address, and hung up. I stared at the phone's handset for a moment before hanging up myself.

The cops could try to trace the number later, but even if they managed to work out a location the phone would probably be in the ocean five minutes from now. The Laughing Man wasn't one to take any chances. He was in the wind. Again.

I picked up my cell and called Dan Evans. It went to voicemail. I tried again. On the third try he picked up. "Are you all right?" he asked sleepily.

I gave him the address. "Get a team over there."

"What am I going to find?"

"A body."

I hung up, dressed, and strapped on my Glock, then went outside. The address the Laughing Man had given me was in Ocean Beach. I'd be there before Dan and anyone else he was going to roust for this could make the drive. A voice in my head whispered to me that this could be a trap; maybe *this* was the game the Laughing Man had waited so long to play. But he'd never have done it this way. He'd think of it as cheating.

The address turned out to be that of an elementary school I'd probably passed a hundred times back when I'd lived in Ocean Beach, but had never paid much attention to. I wasn't surprised to find a side door unlocked. It led into a long hallway with classroom doors on either side. The fluorescent lights overhead were on, but only every third light was illuminated. It made the hallway dim and full of shadows, but there was enough light to see by.

I took the Glock out of its holster and held it by my side, then started down the hall. Each classroom door had a rectangular Plexiglas screen above the handle. I looked through the first one and saw only an empty classroom with desks and chairs. The same was true of the next two. The fourth classroom I came to had a light on inside. I looked through the Plexiglas and a chill ran down my spine. This was what I'd come here for.

The classroom door was unlocked. I opened it and went inside, letting it swing shut behind me. I hadn't been in a room like this in ages, but it was more or less what I'd have expected to see. Twenty small desks were laid out in a four-by-five square facing a larger teacher's desk and a blackboard. A row of cubbyholes for jackets and bags stood against the wall near the door. And in the rear of the classroom, in the corner, sat a man on a plastic chair with his back to me. A conical paper hat about two feet tall sat on his head. He wasn't moving. I already knew he wasn't ever going to move again.

I took a step closer, noting that the man's hands and feet had been lashed to the chair to keep his body in place. His forehead was just barely touching the wall. Part of me knew I should wait, and through the classroom window I could see red lights flashing now. The cops would be inside any second. I wanted to have a look for myself first, though. He'd been placed here for me to find, after all. It seemed like something I should do.

The word "dunce" had been printed in block letters on the dead man's paper hat. Looking closer, I could see that the hat had been stapled into place on the man's head. The Laughing Man hadn't wanted to risk it falling off and ruining his piece.

I put a hand on the back of the man's head and pulled it back. His eyes were still open, but his lips were gone and the skin sliced perfectly back toward the ears to form the wide smile the Laughing Man carved into all his victims. It was Brad Ellis, just as I'd known it would be the moment my phone rang back at the motel. I wondered if the Laughing Man had figured it out before Sarah had. Maybe. That was something I could ask him the next time we met.

I put Ellis's head back against the wall and went to sit at the teacher's desk. The cops would be inside any second now. Dan would barge in here like a charging elephant and I'd be getting a barrage of "are you okay" questions for the next few days. I'd probably have cops staking out my motel with detectives hoping the Laughing Man would put in an appearance. He wouldn't, of course, and eventually I'd get sick of the constant surveillance and move.

I could hear voices in the hallway now. I put my elbows on the desk and tented my fingers. What should I do next? After the questions that would be coming, anyway. I was no closer to the Laughing Man than I had been three months ago. The game hadn't started; this was just a distraction he'd wanted to get out of the way. When were we going to finally *play*, for God's sake?

They said patience was a virtue. I'd never been much good at it. But I'd wait. I'd wait, and I'd watch, and one of these days it would be game over.

One of us was going to die when that happened. I knew that. The Laughing Man knew it, too. And just like me, he knew our last meeting might well mean the end of both of us.

The truth was, I didn't care. As long as I took him with me, it would be worth it.

Come on, I thought. *Let's play.*

ALSO BY MATTHEW STORM

The Interesting Times Series

Interesting Times
Interesting Places

Nevada James Mysteries

Broken
Scars

The Riley Flynn Series (as M.J. Storm)

Riley Flynn and the Runaway Fairy

ABOUT THE AUTHOR

Matthew Storm lives in Anchorage, Alaska.